GURL TALK AT THE SHOP

AT THE

SHOP

Dirty Little Secrets

GURL TALK AT THE SHOP

Dirty Little Secrets

JADE BADD & RENEE LOVE

GURL TALK PUBLICATIONS

PUBLICATIONS

Published by Gurl Talk Publications
P.O. Box 442502 Fort Washington, MD 20749

Library of Congress Cataloging-in-Publications Data

www.gurltalkpublications.com

ISBN **978-0692481356**

Dedication

This book is dedicated to our families, friends, supporters and all the dreamers of the world. We truly appreciate each of you! Many continued blessings.

Acknowledgments

A huge thanks to…

Our Heavenly Father for all of your favor, gifts and blessings. You brought the right people in our path at the right time. We know none of this would be possible without you.

Our loving husbands for encouraging us along the way. There were a lot of long nights and you guys were there pushing us along to see our dream become a reality.

Our beautiful children for believing in us and giving us something to dream for.

Our parents for everything! You guys raised two independent driven women. You all served as the best examples and for that we can't thank you enough.

Dex H. Wood, our editor: For being patient with us along this journey. You are the best! You are part of our family for life. Love and appreciate you!

Natasha Brown: For your wisdom, insight and encouragement.

Shakila: We adore you, beautiful. You always believed in this project and we can't thank you enough for being a true friend.

Kandace: Love you sis! They don't make them like you no more.

Laryssa: You stay grinding diva and we thank you for all your positive words and encouragement.

Krysten Joi, Tahayah Lewis, and Dyrec: We appreciate you guys so much for holding us down. I see nothing but big things in all of your futures. Grammy awards and all that…

Our Southern Sounds Films Family: There aren't enough words to express how much we appreciate you guys. Much love! We had so much fun, it didn't feel like work. Forward to our next project.

Our Reflexion Dominican Salon Family: You divas rock! We can't thank you all enough for always being there when we needed you. Much respect!!

Our graphics team: William A. Brown, Kendrick Ware, Traci Baker, Melissa Duncan, Mickey Freeman and Chrishawn: You guys are amazing! You all truly brought our vision out with the cover, photographs, website and all promotional materials.

If we missed anybody blame it on our heads and not our hearts. We appreciate everyone for supporting us, and spreading the word. …Muah!!

Table of Contents

Intro

"Let me see your appointment book, girl. Remember, I'm having my divorce party next Friday, so I need to be in your chair to get right. I want to make sure all of Tommy's friends and family run tell how fabulous I look. I'm going to flood their timelines on Facebook and most certainly will be on Instagram, straight flexing. I especially want that home-wrecker Kim to see. You know I posted those nude pictures of her on Facebook that I found in Tommy's phone when we were together. Take a look girl...just look at those saggy titties."

"Shut up. Rachel Denise! Haven't you any shame? You tell all your business to Jade. She is just your stylist and not a therapist, you know." I laugh as I overhear one of my bougie clients, Lisa, get on her sister, Rachel, about telling me all of her private affairs. I pause from the weave install I'm diligently working on, and turn around to say, "Honey don't you know it's nothing more than just a little „Gurl Talk at the Shop!'"

The Shop, also known as the hair salon, is a place where women go to get away from the stress of life. To relax, get pampered, and to get their hair laid. But let's not forget, we go to have gurl talk, as well. Many of my clients do indeed call me their therapist as I keep their most ridiculous secrets confidential and always offer great advice. Not because I have to, but because I want to. Where else can you go that has all of that in one place?

My name is Jade. My cousin Renee and I own one of the most popular salons in the Washington, DC metropolitan area, also known as the DMV. The name of my salon is Sweet Styles, and my motto is, "Give your hair a sweet treat, it's just dessert." I believe we all deserve to treat ourselves, and our hair, sometimes. Giving your hair a delicious style is the only dessert that is guaranteed to be kind to your waist.

My salon is located in the middle of a busy shopping center and definitely catches the eyes of many. Not only for its sexy, and modern design, but also for the fabulous styles and divas that walk in and out of the place. I have all types of beautiful bombshells as clients—from high-paid executives, to strippers and grandmas. Yes, women from all walks of life, and every shape, size and color. There is no discriminating or judgment here. All are welcome to the shop, to unwind, vent and get glamorous. My stylists and I are here to serve.

As soon as you walk through the salon's frosted glass doors, you feel invited and welcome. The receptionist, Omani, sits in the center of the entrance and greets everyone with her beautiful smile. Omani is Jamaican and has flawless brown skin. The girl is bad and always rocks the latest styles in hair and fashion. I call her my business' walking billboard. Her desk is always neat and is black and charcoal gray, with a unique oblong design. This plays off the colors of my shop, which are white, black and silver. The white and gray marbled floors give it a touch of class.

I put a lot of time and money into my salon and recently installed a five-tier Swarovski crystal chandelier that trickles down over the waiting area shining and sparkling with the beautiful colors of the crystals that light up from the bulbs and beams of sunlight. I really wanted to give the place that "wow factor!"

There are six stylists, including myself; a massage therapist; manicurist; and three shampoo assistants. Every day in my shop is a fashion, hair, and talk show, always featuring our regulars, special guests, and pop-up appearances by some longtime missing-in-action clients. And oh yes, from time to time we do get a few wild cards in the bunch.

Stylists are considered miracle workers, in some cases, magicians. You can come in the salon with seven strands of hair, but leave out with a head full. Voila! Just like magic! And, as stated earlier, stylists, for some, are considered a part-time therapist. Clients feel comfortable around their stylist because they feel they can trust them with their crown and glory. Hair is such an important part of our appearance. We can be very protective and particular about our hair, so we have to form a bond of trust with the person who we choose to leave it in the hands of. That's why a lot of clients vent to their stylist and tell them what they're going through, and sometimes they even tell some of their "Dirty Little Secrets." We can be there for each other by being a set of ears to listen, a set of eyes to see and witness, and a mouth to speak advice and opinions.

Believe me, though, not everything is always peachy. Some discussions turn into disagreements, some disagreements turn into heated debates and almost physical altercations. But luckily for my shop, arguments quickly get resolved and shut down. I don't tolerate a whole lot of foolishness. There are only a few times that I can remember having had to make someone leave because of unruly behavior. But it has happened.

In the shop we have discussions about everything from A to Z. Relationships, politics, nightlife, restaurants, our children; haters, strippers, cars, fashion, and who's hot and who's not. You name it we talk about it—especially when it comes to sex! Who's doing whom and, of course, how they doin' it! That's right, sometimes the tea must be spilled, honey. So read these short stories that are full of intimate encounters, intrigue, romance, seduction, betrayal, excitement, and some that are straight-out naughty. We bond together in the shop and offer encouragement and support, helpful hints on technique, as well as a good laugh or a needed hug. We share stories whether good or bad, love or lust, tears from hurt emotions, or from the joys of laughing too hard. Through all of the years that I've been a stylist, I have gone through a lot, seen a lot, and I have definitely heard a lot. Some of the stories seem too crazy to be true, and some of the stories can be relatable to a personal experience that you or someone that you know may have had. Take your time, relax. I guarantee you won't regret it! But remember, you didn't hear it from me. ...Wink.

Take One for the Team

Aja is one of my favorite clients. I have been styling her for years. She is truly beautiful and blessed, and she tips well, but lately I noticed her tips are even better. With this story she told me, I now know why. ...I must admit I was a little disappointed in her at first, but who am I to judge? ...

It was another long day on the job for Aja when she was called into her supervisor's office; little did she know she was in for a pleasant surprise. Her supervisor, Dottie, said Aja's suitemate Dominique was not able to attend the Blacks in Engineering conference in New Orleans due to a death in the family. Dottie wanted to know if Aja would like to attend in Dominique's place. Aja was thrilled. Of course, she felt bad for Dominique's loss, but she was excited to get a chance to attend the conference. Their firm was one of the top engineering companies in the country, and she had worked there for five years, but had never got a chance to go on travel. She had felt passed over many times. She knew she couldn't let this opportunity pass her by.

Dottie said the trip required Aja to leave tomorrow, so she said she would understand if Aja couldn't make it. Aja was married to a powerful divorce attorney, who worked longer hours than Aja and liked for her to be home right where he could count on her to take care of the home front. Additionally, they had three small children. Aja quickly responded yes to Dottie's invitation. However, in the back of her mind she knew her husband John would have a problem. But this was her time to finally get some time to herself. She knew she could always ask her sister to watch the kids if all else failed. Aja walked out of Dottie's office with the biggest smile. She immediately walked over to the administrative assistant's desk to have her travel arrangements made.

"Whew, 5:30 has finally arrived. It's quitting time!!" Aja exclaimed, and then stopped past Dottie's office on the way out the building to again express her appreciation. Dottie was happy that Aja could travel on such short notice and said, "You better get going so you're ready for your big trip tomorrow. Please bring me back some beignets, heavy powder." Aja promised and headed out. She quickly hopped in her Lexus RX 350 and got on her phone to call John to inform him of the trip. To her surprise John was supportive; he even offered to ask his mom to watch the kids and relieve her of her mommy duties even for that night. She then could take her time getting home since he was sure she wanted to get her hair and nails done before leaving for the Big Easy tomorrow.

Everything seemed to be too good to be true. Aja got her man's blessing, got an appointment with her stylist and was ready to get fly for the conference. On the way to the salon, Aja stopped off at Nordstrom to pick up a couple of suits. She knew the engineering conference was a big deal. She knew she could network and meet other possible employers. Don't get it twisted; Aja didn't want to be a worker-bee forever. Her dream was to one day open her own engineering firm. However, she knew she had to work for someone first to save enough money to open her own business. Aja was twenty-eight, but had big dreams. She had always been a dreamer. Aja planned her life out at an early age and, thus far, had met all of her goals. Just as written in her middle-school yearbook, she got her undergrad degree in business administration from Morgan State and received her engineering degree from Howard. She was a go-getter and no one could stop her.

After running errands and getting beautified at the salon, it was close to midnight when Aja finally pulled into her driveway. She unlocked the front door and was welcomed by two of her favorite people in the world—John, and John's huge cock, Peter. Yes, "Peter"—that was the name Aja gave John's manhood. John was Irish but was hung like a horse. Aja grew up on her grandmother's farm in

Georgia and had a horse named Peter. When she was little she remembered how huge Peter the horse's cock was. Aja and her cousins would giggle whenever Peter's cock would come out. When Aja and John started dating she didn't know what it would be like to be with a white man, but when they became intimate and she felt that huge cock she knew it would work. She immediately named and claimed John's member or "joy stick" as Peter.

"My chocolate Godiva queen, go upstairs and enjoy the hot bubble bath I prepared for you," John said. Aja smiled with delight while looking at her fine blue-eyed partner, and his big friend playing hide and seek between the slit in his boxers. Aja's mind wandered, but came back quickly and she complied and soaked in the tub. Her smooth, chocolate skin shined as she got out. Aja, as John had indeed proclaimed, had the body of a Goddess. She was a statuette five feet ten inches with a tiny waist and huge behind, and her smooth, bronzed skin looked like she was dipped in Hershey's chocolate. John was naked in their bed waiting for her. Aromatherapy candles were lit and warm massage oil ready. He said softly, seductively, "Come bring your beautiful body over to this bed, so I can give you something to remember on your business trip." That night Aja and John made love for hours, creating the ultimate swirl.

The alarm startled the lovers at 6:00 a.m. After a few moments of barely realizing where she was, Aja remembered it was time for her to get up and head out for the Big Easy. She quickly showered and dressed, kissed John (and Peter), then grabbed her bags and headed out to Thurgood Marshall BWI Airport. She had butterflies in her stomach as she waited for her flight to be called.

Because this was Aja's first time on business travel, she wanted to make good connections and make the most of her trip. She looked around the terminal wondering if any of the folks waiting were also attending the conference. While waiting she heard a familiar voice in the distance. She turned to see and it was her son's classmate's mother, Joann. Aja smiled in delight to see a familiar face. Joann stopped her conversation with the elderly couple sitting next to her and walked over to Aja. They embraced and said "Hey girl" in unison. They laughed, and Joann said, "I'm going to yet another boring conference. Girl, I swear my job sends me on all the office trips."

Joann was Creole so she was light skinned, with green eyes and dark brown curly hair. She had a body like a video vixen and a style like none other. Joann stayed Gucci and YSL draped; she truly oozed swag. Joann mentioned that she was happy to go on this trip because she was going to her hometown of New Orleans. Aja was super excited and asked Joann if she was going to the engineering conference? She said yes. Aja responded, "Me too, girlie!! Yes, I'm so happy to have someone to hang with in New Orleans." Aja was thrilled that Joann was from the Crescent City, and she probably would know of all the hot spots to venture to during the conference.

The ladies laughed and shared stories about their little ones until it was time to board the plane. When they landed in New Orleans they immediately met up to walk to baggage claim and they even shared a cab to their hotels. Joann mentioned that she wasn't able to link up that evening because she needed to spend family time with her grandmother and aunt. She said most of her family had left New Orleans after Hurricane Katrina, so it was only her grandma and auntie, along with a few cousins, who remained. She was proud of her Creole culture and taught Aja a few Creole words before arriving to Joann's hotel. They hugged and promised to meet up in the morning at the first session. The cab drove on to where Aja was staying.

Aja was in deep thought as her cab arrived at the W Hotel. She was impressed with the plush red entrance, and the bellmen were warm and welcoming. Aja quickly checked in and got settled in her room. She called John and his mom to check on the family and kids. Everyone was good. So Aja decided to roam the city on her own this beautiful first day in the Big Easy. She took a riverboat tour, which she greatly enjoyed; the tour included a meal with authentic Louisiana-style food—shrimp, oysters, crawfish, gumbo, all that. Aja fell in love with the food, smells and sounds of New Orleans. After the tour she decided to head down to the famous French Market, which had all types of vendors, even one that sold fresh gator. Being the explorer she was, Aja bought some to nibble and to her surprise, liked it. On the way back to the W Hotel, Aja went to Café du Monde for some coffee and beignets. She had to go there to see what all the fuss was about. Everyone who knew she was going to New Orleans had asked her to bring back some beignets. Now she understood why; they were so delicious. Aja felt like she was in heaven, and was so thankful to be able to have gotten away. She looked down at her Gucci watch and realized it was 8:45 p.m. She couldn't believe how fast her first day in New Orleans had gone by. After her full day, it was time to head back to the hotel and get ready for tomorrow. After all, she was there to learn and make contacts at the conference.

When Aja's taxi pulled up to the W Hotel, she noticed there were dozens of exotic cars lined up. There were Bentleys, Aston Martins and limos. She paid the taxi driver and headed towards the entrance of her hotel. In the lobby of the W there were tons of people. She didn't know what was going on so she asked the bellman that helped her earlier. He said some of the players for the New Orleans Saints were hosting a party. Aja secretly wished she could go but just kept heading towards the elevators. As she walked several guys looked and flirted. Remember, Aja is a bad ebony chick, and she knew it. She just smiled and played it cool. There was some eye candy in the building, but Aja thought, naw, let me get in my room and be good. As she snapped back to reality on her way to the elevator, a huge funny looking dark-skinned guy with bad skin and a blinged-out grill, approached with his boys, and said, "Hey, sexy chocolate."

Aja looked and smiled not because she liked what she saw, but in amusement that this guy thought he had a chance. The huge monster said, "Hey there, gah. Won't cha join me and my boys, we having a party at the penthouse?"

Aja flashed her beautiful smile and quickly declined. He became annoyed, and smacked her ass, while also grabbing her arm, saying, "Look gal, you must not know who I am. I am the new quarterback, in fact, the hottest in the league, and I can buy this hotel, including you babes."

Aja's niceness quickly wore off. She snapped, and in a politically correct way said, "Brother, I don't care who you are, I have my own and am not a typical chicken-head who is excited by your bling. Now, I advise you to get your dirty hands off me before I call my lawyer. Or better yet, scream and make a scene." She added, "I respect your game but not your approach." He quickly let go and she remarked, "Thank you. I'm glad we have an understanding. Enjoy your night, monster." His boys looked on in amazement, laughed and jokingly called their teammate "monster."

Aja walked into the elevator, overwhelmed by her actions and independence. She felt good to be by herself and to take up for herself. She hurried to her room, took off her Gucci tennis shoes and undressed. She took a warm shower and slept like a baby.

The morning quickly arrived and Aja pulled out her favorite Ann Taylor suit for the first day of the conference. She took a cab and met Joann in the lobby of the Marriott, which was the location of the event. They mixed and mingled all day. Going from session to session, taking notes and networking, the ladies were really making moves. The end of the day arrived and they were ready to enjoy the spicy city's nightlife. They both wanted to head back to their rooms to change clothes and freshen up. They agreed to meet at Ruth Chris' promptly at 8 p.m. for dinner.

Ruth Chris was right around the corner from the W Hotel, so Aja walked over, and was greeted promptly by Joann. The ladies both looked fly, and Aja jokingly said, "We're vanilla and chocolate dime-divas doing it big in the Big Easy." Joann had on a short colorful dress with some gold Christian Louboutin sandals and Aja had on all white, with her skinny white jeans hugging her curves just right. She had on her favorite silver Versace heels and was feeling like a million bucks. In fact, the shoe games of both ladies were sick. As they walked in they noticed three nice looking guys starring at them like they were on the dinner menu. The ladies both took notice and laughed like two schoolgirls, and the hostess sat them.

Their waiter was a handsome Creole guy named John Paul. He and Joann clicked right away and spoke Creole. Aja just looked in the distance like, OK enough. The waiter broke his chatter with Joann to say those guys over there said you ladies can order whatever you like and its totally on them. They looked back and it was the three guys from when they first walked in. Aja said, "OK, tell them we want a bottle of Dom P." Joann burst into laughter and said, "Yes, please tell them we want a bottle." The waiter laughed too and said OK. A few seconds later the three guys walked over and one of the guys said "Sweethearts, we were serious when we said you can order whatever you like. Your bottle of Dom P is on its way over. Anything else you want you can have."

He was fine as wine. He had silky dark skin, a flawless complexion and perfect smile. The brother was smooth and his gang was too. They all had on Christian Louboutin shoes and were dressed to impress. They introduced themselves, the dark-skinned smooth guy said his name was Andre, Joe was his brother and their cousin went by the name of Slim. Joe and Slim were fine too. They both were caramel with beautiful skin and wavy black hair. Aja and Joann were all smiles. Andre did all the talking. He looked directly into Aja's eyes and said, "Look, we saw some beautiful queens enter Ruth Chris and we just wanted to make sure you ladies enjoyed yourselves. We got to go back to our table to finish our meals, but we liked what we saw and knew we had to meet you. Ladies enjoy, and remember order whatever you like. I got you." Andre and the other fly guys walked back over to their table, looking like some fine models straight out of the pages of GQ magazine. They were some official dudes; Aja and Joann were thoroughly impressed. They giggled and laughed just full of excitement from meeting them.

Joann was quiet for a minute and said, "Girl, you know, what did that guy say his name was again? You know the dark-skinned brother." Aja said, "Andre; his name is Andre."

Joann said, "Wow! I think I know him. I think he might be this big baller from back in the day. Don't quote me, but he looks like this dude that used to run the streets, girl. OMG! I don't know about him girl. I heard some stories about him and his crew. They some ballers, but we grown women with kids—I ain't trying to get caught up."

Aja didn't pay Joann any attention; she told her, "Whatever. I'm going to enjoy this free meal and bottle of Dom P." The waiter popped the bottle of Dom Perignon champagne and the ladies enjoyed their lobster. Andre walked over right when the ladies were discussing their next move. He gave Aja his card and said call me. He said he and his boys were about to go down to Bourbon Street to this party. "You ladies are more than welcome to join us," he said, adding, "I would love to show you girls a good time." He then asked where they were from, and made other small talk. His cousin and brother walked over. Joe and Slim both fought for Joann's attention. She smiled, giggled and enjoyed every moment of their flirtation. Andre and Aja connected instantly, he was impressed by her lady-like qualities, education and drive. The waiter came by and thanked Andre for the huge tip. Andre pulled out a $100 bill and said, "Naw, brother, *thank you*, for coming back for your appreciation." The waiter was too thrilled. Andre said, "Look ladies, come on, y'all may as well come out with us tonight."

Joann looked like she quickly changed her mind about hanging with Andre and his crew; she gave Aja a look like, hell yeah, let's go. Andre said, "You ladies can ride with me, I got my Hummer." They all walked up front for the valet. Joe got in his drop-top Mercedes and headed home. He said he had to get some rest but gave Joann a long goodnight hug, and then slid her his number. She smiled and hopped in the Hummer. Slim said, "Man, throw Joe's number away. I'm the one, baby." Aja, riding copilot, burst into laughter at Slim's strong Louisiana accent as he said baby this and baby that. Aja also noticed just how fly Andre was. She was caught off guard by her sudden attraction. She had been with John so long she really didn't notice other men. Andre caught Aja looking hard at him and smiled. He asked, "What you thinking about, beautiful?"

"Nothing. Just wondering where you are taking us," Aja responded.

"Don't worry. You want to have a good time, right?"

"Right," Aja nodded.

"OK, trust me. Slim and I are going to take good care of you ladies. We gonna show you why people love New Orleans."

Joann quickly chimed in and said, "Well, show me something 'cause I'm from here and haven't been back since Katrina. Most of the spots I used to frequent are closed."

The white Hummer pulled up to this hot spot called the Metropolitan Nightclub. As soon as they arrived, a valet dapped Andre up and opened the vehicle's doors. The ladies skipped the line with Andre and walked right in. Once inside it felt like they were in the middle of a video shoot, folks were dancing, drinks were flowing and the music was on point. The club owner walked up to Andre with a huge smile full of bling and said, "We got your section all ready for you, man." We followed Andre and Slim to the VIP section where a bucket of Dom P and Rosé waited for us. Andre hoisted the bottle of Dom P and laughed, "Yeah, ladies. I called in advance to make sure your favorite was chilled for you."

Aja and Joann looked at each other and laughed. Joann raised a glass and Slim poured her some Dom as they danced and flirted. Aja was sipping on some Rosé when she noticed the monster from the night before walking over. He didn't notice Aja right away; he seemed to be coming over to speak to Andre. The football player and Andre were in deep conversation when the monster noticed Aja. "Hey, hey there miss lady. Don't I know you?"

Aja said, "Of course you do. I'm your friend from last night. Remember?" The monster looked at Andre and said, "Oh, man, this your peeps? Wow! Dude, your gal ain't know who I was, man. She's a real chick. I likes shorty, dawg. How you get her on your team?"

Andre just laughed and said don't worry bout all that, and he quickly moved onto another subject. Aja decided to get up and walk around, leaving the VIP area and going to the bar to buy a drink. She wanted to distance herself from the monster and his goons, who had brought a number of THOTS with them into Andre's VIP section. Yeah, there were plenty of drinks flowing in VIP, all on Andre. But Aja wanted to enjoy herself, and moved onto the dance floor. It wasn't long before she felt a solid frame behind her. She looked back and it was Andre. He whispered in her ear, "You alright beautiful?" Aja said yes. He then asked why she had left his VIP booth. She explained the situation she had experienced with the football player the night before. He shook his head and said, "That sounds like that ignorant ass; he's a client of mine." Andre took Aja's hand and walked her back over to VIP where things had cleared out. Slim, Joann and a few others were in the section partying. Andre smoothly placed his hands around Aja's waist and began to dance with her. They danced the night through and shut down the club.

As they were leaving, Andre stopped in his tracks and said to Joann and Slim that he needed to speak privately to Aja for a minute. He pulled her aside and said, "Man, I want you bad. I know you are married, and all. But look, I'm well off and will do anything to have a taste of you. Whatever it takes, I don't care. You know, I own an exotic car rental company and several other businesses. I have millions, lady, and want to have you."

Aja was shocked and said, "Sorry, but didn't your football friend tell you I'm not for sell? I see you're just like the rest."

"No, really I'm not, they want to take you shopping or to dinner. I want to change your life. Seriously, is there anything you need—a house, a business, whatever? Look I like your style. You're a lady and mad intelligent. I can see something in you."

Aja laughed and said, "I'm sure you can see something in me, like your dick."

They both laughed and walked off. Then he said softly, "Seriously, think about it." It was 4 a.m. Both Aja and Joann wanted to know how they were going to make it through the conference, which was about to start in a few hours.

On the ride back to their hotels, Joann and Aja both thanked the guys for a fun night. Joann said, "Man I'm glad to see my hometown still knows how to party. Whoa!!!"

Andre and Slim were thrilled for them to have had such as good night. Andre said, "Well, ladies, if you all don't have plans, let's get together again tomorrow, oops I mean tonight. I promise not to keep y'all up too late. I can have one of my drivers come pick y'all up in one of my exotic stretch cars. I want you all to see the lower ninth ward. Y'all got to see how good of a job our elected officials have done with the rebuilding effort. Plus, I just want to enjoy y'all's company again. You had everyone in the club asking me and Slim about y'all, man."

Joann answered for both her and Aja, saying, "Hell yeah. Let's do it again. Y'all know I'm from here but haven't been back since 2005. I want to see what's going down in my city. My nana and auntie still here, and they been telling me how much its changed."

Slim said, "Baby, you know I got to ask, if you one of dem Creole girls?"

Joann's face lit up. She loved telling everyone about her Creole heritage. "Yes, indeed. What you know about us Creole girls? We da best, you know. What they say, „If she looks that good she got to be Creole?'" She added, "No offense Aja, I can't help myself sometimes. Anyway your babies look Creole."

Aja rolled her eyes and looked out the window; she hated people with color complexes. Joann was a little tipsy and was getting loud. Aja was so happy that Joann was first to get dropped off. She enjoyed being around Joann, but she had enough of her for the night. As Joann was getting ready to exit the car she hollered, "I can't wait until tonight. Y'all showed this NOLA Creole gal a good time."

She gave Slim a kiss on the cheek goodnight and did a sexy walk to her hotel's entrance.

As they drove off Andre said, "Man, Aja, I really enjoyed hanging with you and your friend tonight. You are my kind of lady."

Aja laughed and said, "What does that mean?"

He kissed her on the forehead and said, "I have a serious chocolate addiction. It's something about that smooth dark skin. Damn, and your conversation is on another level. I like you. You are perfect, it's crazy 'cause you are exactly my type," adding, "I don't say that too often so believe me." Aja was not naïve by any means. She recognized game, but there was something about the way Andre said what he said to her that felt real and genuine.

When they pulled in front of her hotel, Andre got out the car and walked Aja to the hotel entrance. He held her tight and said, softly, "I got to have you. Whatever it takes to get with you I don't care. Seriously, I mean that."

Aja smiled and said, "I hear you, we shall see."

"OK, Andre said, "I like a challenge, so again, whatever it takes."

A million thoughts ran through Aja's head. She just said, "Andre I got to get up in a couple of hours. Let's enjoy each other further later tonight." Andre agreed and watched Aja walk to the elevator doors.

Andre was really feeling Aja and called her shortly after dropping her off. He asked if he could come back and spend time with her. Aja was silent for a minute and she went back and forth with the question of should I or shouldn't I let him come back. She looked at the picture of her family on the hotel nightstand and said, "No, let's just link up tonight as planned. All that dancing tonight got a sister tired."

Andre said, "OK, you gave me something to look forward to." They chatted for about an hour about everything, from how he made his first million to politics. Come to find out, Andre was highly educated. He graduated top of his class from Stanford. He hung with the thugs back in his teen years, but turned things around when his cousin was murdered their senior year of high school. Aja was really impressed with Andre and even had a dream about him that night.

Ring, ring, ring. …Aja looked at the alarm clock. It was 6:43 a.m. She cursed whoever was calling her at this hour. Heck she had just lied down to go to sleep. She picked up. It was perky Joann. "Good morning, sunshine! You ready to work out?"

Aja said, "Girl, bye. I can't do this today. I'll meet you at the conference at 8:00."

Joann said, "Hold up. You ain't getting off that easy. What happened after I got dropped off? Andre is feeling you girl. What happened?"

Aja said, "OK, I get it. You called me this early because you couldn't wait to hear about what happened with me, and my new boo. Well, girl, I feel bad. We got it in. He broke my back last night girl."

"I know that's right," Joann said.

"No, I was just playing with you, crazy. Nothing happened. He just talked that talk—you know, telling me he would do anything to have me," Aja laughed.

"Well, girl. You know Andre is powerful and a millionaire. He probably means every word he says. You might have to take one for the team, Aja."

Aja didn't get it. "What are you saying, „Take one for the team?'"

Joann clarified: "Well, you know your dreams of opening your own engineering firm and how I want to be your partner? Getting with Andre can make that happen. I know he would support your dream, girl. Take one for the team so we can come up. I know you're saving money each month so you can open your business but that can take years. Andre's money can make it happen—now."

Aja sat up in the bed and thought about what Joann had said. She was a little upset at first but now she said to herself, "Brilliant, I can do this." She just didn't let Joann know her thoughts right away. She just listened as Joann provided a million reasons why Aja should come up by letting Andre have a taste.

Aja went back to acting like she was tired and said, "Girl, I hear you. But let's talk about this further over lunch. I'm tired and ready to get some more ZZZZs."

"OK, but don't be late to the conference."

The two ladies hung up.

Aja was far from tired now. The idea of having her own firm was heavy on her mind. She looked at her family picture and cried. She said, how could I even think like this? What would John say if he ever found out? But she quickly snapped back to her business sense and put the picture away. She said aloud to herself, "Yeah, I'm going to take one for the team, like Joann said. The team also includes my family. With me having my own firm, I can call all the shots. At first I know it will take a lot of work to get things running but once established it can change our entire lifestyle." Aja made her decision and was comfortable with it. She laid back down to get her rest in for a long day ahead and an even longer night.

At the conference, Aja had a hard time concentrating. All she could think about was Andre and how far he was willing to go to get what he wanted. In every session, she daydreamed about how she would present information at next year's conference on behalf of her firm. That is, if she played her cards right. …

The day seemed to quickly pass and Aja was ready to have another fun-filled night. She met Joann in the lobby after the day's last session. "I'm ready to hang tonight girl," Joann said, and quickly added, "Have you spoken to Andre, yet?" Aja said no. Surprisingly, Joann hadn't brought up Andre's proposition all day.

Aja decided it was time to check in with him, and pulled out her cell phone. Andre picked up on the second ring, and Aja and Andre exchanged small talk. Then he asked if Joann and Aja were still available to hangout that night. Aja said yes, as Joann grinned hard, listening-in on the call. They made plans to meet and everything was all set for the evening.

Aja hung up and she and Joann jumped up and down like two high-school girls that had been asked out by two football captains. They left the conference and headed back to their hotel rooms to freshen up and get ready for a fun-filled night.

But Aja's excitement was about to truly fly off the charts. When she opened the door to her room, she was totally caught off guard. There were ten-dozen white roses and three beautifully wrapped presents sitting there. She instantly thought it was a mistake, and called down to the front desk. The desk clerk confirmed that there was no mix up. The young lady must have been there when the flowers and gifts arrived because she was so expressive. In her thick

Louisiana accent she said, "Baby, I saw dem there flowers come in and I lost my mind. My coworkers and I talked about that for hours. You must be a beauty. Enjoy, baby."

Aja hung up the phone and sat on her bed, taking it all in before jumping to conclusions. She wondered if these gifts were from her loving husband John or from Andre. She searched the roses for a card. There was nothing. Then, as she grabbed one of the beautifully wrapped presents, a card dropped. *"You are truly a queen and a queen deserves nothing but the best. This is just the beginning of what I will do to have a taste of you. Andre Johnson."*

John was a sweetheart, but Aja hadn't been spoiled like this in years. Andre's plan was working. Aja opened the presents: In the first box was a pair of Christian Louboutins; the second box contained a beautiful animal print Dior dress; and the third box was a *bad* Gucci clutch with a Gucci watch and earrings. Aja was *soooo* excited. She quickly tried on her new outfit and looked and felt like a star. She took some pictures with her camera phone and sent them to Joann. She also took pictures of her rose-filled room. Joann called so fast…

"Please. Tell me Andre did not do that?!"

"Yes, Andre did this."

Joann screamed, "Damn, girl! What you do to him? Keep it real—you already gave him „a little something he could feel' last night after you dropped me off?"

"No girl," Aja laughed. "We did nothing. He hasn't even seen me naked, yet."

"Damn, why his cousin or brother ain't send me no flowers? Let me look in my closet," Joann said.

They both laughed and continued with small talk. Andre beeped Aja's other line and she told Joann she'd call her back. Aja answered, "Thank you so much for the surprise."

"Baby girl, I keep trying to tell you, if you rock with me you get nothing but the best," Andre said. "Girl, I been thinking about you all day and wanted to show you how serious I am about how much I'm feeling you."

"I see," Aja replied, and whispered to Andre, "I want to show you my appreciation tonight." For now, she said, she wanted to lie down to take a nap. They hung up. She called Joann back, told her she was going to rest and for her to be ready tonight.

Eight o'clock quickly came. Around that time, Aja got a call from Andre stating that a stretch Mercedes Benz would be coming to pick her and Joann up. Aja was shocked but loved the idea of receiving such special treatment. She said to herself, first the gifts, now I'm getting picked up in a stretch Mercedes. Wow! She quickly showered and put on her new items from Andre. The Dior dress hugged Aja's curves, oh so perfectly. She really looked like a queen. Aja's phone rang and it was an unfamiliar number. She picked up and it was the limo driver saying he was downstairs. Aja was on her way. And when she walked in the elevator and out into the lobby, all eyes were on her. She knew she looked good as she approached the stretch white Benz; the chauffeur opened the door and introduced himself. Aja looked in and noticed that Andre wasn't there. The chauffeur said, "Aja, how are you? My name is Jack. Andre wanted me to let you know he'll be meeting you later. They got held up with a client."

Jack got in the car and they headed over to pick up Joann. Of course, Joann acted a fool when she saw the car. She didn't get in without first having the chauffeur take pictures of her in front of the limo. Aja was getting a little frustrated as the photo shoot was getting too involved—it took about ten minutes. Joann finally got in and began singing, "You fancy, huh."…The ladies both laughed. Soon, Jack interrupted and asked, "Where would you ladies like to go." They both looked at each other with a puzzled look. They said well Andre mentioned he was going to take us to the ninth ward, do you think you can take us there? Jack said, "Yes, I'll take you ladies wherever you want to go." Joann quickly asked where the fellas were and Aja filled her in.

As they arrived to the ninth ward the girls hearts sank as they saw the devastation Katrina left behind. Most houses were still a wreck. Jack explained that even though many year's later, nothing had been done to help most of those who had lived in the area. He drove past one cleared spot and said, "This was my grandma's house—at least we think this is where it was." All that was there now were some steps. The ladies looked at each other and cried, both knowing how blessed they were to have what they had at home. The drive through the ninth ward was eye opening.

The chauffeur then received a phone call; it was Andre. He asked Jack to ask the ladies where they wanted to go. Aja and Joann had no clue and said in unison, "Surprise us," and Jack rolled up the partition. They rode around for about thirty minutes until they arrived at a beautiful estate. It was gated with all white vehicles in the U-shaped driveway. Joann and Aja just looked at each other and smiled, while trying to keep their game-face on to not appear as if they weren't used to this type of living.

Jack opened Aja's door and said, "Ladies welcome to your destination." The two gorgeous divas walked up to this giant, white double-door home and rang the bell. Joe answered the door and greeted the girls with a warm hug. "Since you ladies couldn't decide on where to have dinner," he said, "Andre and I decided to host you at Andre's crib. Take off your shoes and make yourselves at home."

Joanne was surprised to see Joe, since she had just danced the night away with Slim. But still, they had only danced and hadn't spoken since that night. And Joann was pleased to see Joe again. He was about as smooth as his brother and equally fine. This could be interesting, she thought. The air was filled with the smell of seafood. Joann's big mouth yelled out, "Who is in there cooking; it sure smells good." Aja shot her a look like, girl act like you been somewhere. They glanced at each other and just grinned as they walked into Andre's beautiful white and gray marble two-story foyer.

His home was something out of a magazine, it was so beautifully decorated. Andre was sitting in the living room watching the Redskins and Giants play. He signaled for the girls to come in and have a seat. Aja sat on a couch across from Andre and he kept staring as if to say, girl, get your butt over here.

"What are you looking at," Aja asked demurely, with a smile that glowed.

"The most beautiful thing I have ever seen," he replied.

Aja got up and sat next to him. Joann was getting hungry and turned to Joe and said, "Don't you want to check on the food?" he laughed and said no. Andre quickly chimed in and said his chef, Jacques, was cooking up a nice feast for them. Joann, meanwhile, was nodding for Joe to show her around—she was trying to get him to leave the room with her so they could give Aja and Andre some privacy. But Joe was slow to catch on. Instead everyone sat back and watched the game while waiting for dinner to finish.

Aja looked like she was watching the game but all she could think of was Andre and how good he smelled and looked. She glanced over to him and began playing around with erotic ideas of how she would lay him down. Her thoughts were promptly interrupted with Jacques, the chef, ringing in over the home intercom that dinner was ready. All guests should come to the dining area to be served. Served is what they were—there were two exotic Creole women who hosted them for the evening. They were dressed in classy black bandage dresses, which looked like an item from VIP Divas Boutique or something. The dining room was impressive with its high ceiling and beautiful chandeliers with so much bling sunglasses were required to look at them directly. At the end of the table was a huge bucket that had Black Bottles of Luc Belaire and Rosé for days on ice ready to be enjoyed. One of the servers introduced each dish as the other sat them in front of the guests. There was a total seafood feast full of grilled lobster, shrimp, scallops and gumbo.

Joe turned to Joann and said, "You know, you looking rather good and I know Slim's gonna be real mad, but I'm the one who was looking out for you, baby. I requested gumbo just for you since you have Creole roots." The room was quiet for a minute as all were deeply enjoying their tasty meals. Joe broke out into a song about how good the food was and Andre joined in. Those two had the room laughing. Everyone joked, drank, ate and acted a fool. The table was cleared, then one of the servers reentered the dining room, she had the prettiest red curly hair and green eyes. She asked if they were ready for dessert?

Aja quickly chimed in and said, "I know I am. I sure could go for something warm, creamy and white, with…"

Joann interrupted and said, "Yes, dessert sounds good. Thanks..."

Oh my God! Oh my God, Aja thought to herself. What the hell just came over me?

Joe and Andre looked at each other with a smirk. Aja was so embarrassed. She whispered, "I'm sorry, I guess I had one glass too many."

"No worries," Andre said. "I like a woman who knows exactly what she wants." In front of the entire table, Andre whispered in her ear, "Do you *really* want something warm, creamy, and white." Aja paused and shook her head to signal yes. He grabbed her hand and kissed it. He then turned to Joann and Joe to say, "Aja wants to lie down for a minute. I'm gonna take her upstairs. Joann, make yourself at home. My people will take great care of you. Joe take care of the lady and get her whatever she wants."

Joann liked the sound of that, but also wanted to make sure Aja was OK. She turned and asked, "Aja, do you want me to lay with you? Are you sure you are OK?"

Aja smiled and said, "Girl, I'm good." And with that she gave Joann a wink and popped out of her chair to follow Andre to his bedroom.

Andre led her upstairs to the longest hallway, which led to his bedroom. It was decorated in all white—it even had a white bear-skinned rug, with a white marble fireplace. The fireplace was burning as the dancing flames and the light cast against the white room gave it a sexy feeling. In the background, the sensual sounds of Raheem DeVaughn's "Love Connection" played softly. Andre turned to close the door; as soon as he turned around Aja was right there. She pulled him in close and tongue-kissed him passionately. Andre stopped and asked Aja, "Are you sure you want to do this." She gently grabbed his manhood and said, "Don't stop me before I change my mind; when I said I wanted something warm and creamy, I meant it. I want it all. I want to taste you, feel you, touch you. Have all of you in me." Andre's nature quickly rose and was hard as a rock. The feeling of him growing against her thigh made her pussy throb and she felt the warmness of her juices flowing. She took a step back and said, "So, Dre…"

Andre looked at her and replied, "Oh, I'm Dre now."

She laughed. "Yes, baby. Dre, sit back and relax, because tonight is your night. I just met you but it feels like I have known you for years. In appreciation for the love you have shown me in such a short period of time, I have something I want to share with you."

She walked over to his iPod stand and turned the music up. She then started swaying her hips from side to side to the music. The song now playing was appropriate for what she was about to do. It was Beyonce's "Tonight I Want to Dance For You." Andre's eyes got big and Aja twirled and twerked and exotically moved her body. She slid the beautiful Dior dress off her curvy frame and revealed that she was totally nude. She had nothing under that dress the entire night. She stood there in nothing but the Christian Louboutin's Andre had gifted her with. Her bodacious body drove Andre crazy. He wanted her now, but he let Aja take the lead.

"Sit back and relax," she said, and that is what he did. He watched in amazement. He started thinking how he wished he could just take her away forever, but decided to just enjoy the moment for what it was. He reached into his pocket and took out a big stack of money and threw it in the air, making it rain as if they were in a club. Aja laughed and walked over to give Andre a big hug.

She reached down and grabbed his manhood, checking out the true size. Aja got excited as she felt how large and hard he was. She unzipped his pants and dropped to her knees. She was head to head with his large giant penis. She licked around the head and took him deeply into her mouth. She enjoyed every moan she induced from this strong man. She used both of her hands to please him until there was the presence of the creamy, warm, white stuff she desired and asked for. Andre's body shook as he came.

Andre questioned himself; what had happened? He was embarrassed. He couldn't believe how quickly he came. He walked to his bathroom for a towel and he cleaned himself off. He called Aja and she promptly joined him. Andre stretched his long, sculpted arms out and brought Aja close to him, embracing her intensely. Without notice, he picked her up and sat her on the edge of his tub. Looking deep into her eyes he said now it's my turn for dessert. He kissed her down low, licking and sucking every inch of her wet pussy. Aja's legs quivered, and she softly came. Andre looked up and said, "Damn, you taste good. I had a taste for something warm and creamy, too. Now I want all of you."

Andre led Aja by the hand to his giant super-sized bed and he began kissing her body all over. Aja enjoyed every minute of it, she had a wonderful sex life with John but Andre was amazing. In the background Aja could hear Ciara's song with Ludicrous, "He Loves the Way I Ride It," and she felt inspired. She whispered in Andre's ear, "I'm ready to feel you deep inside me. I want all ten inches of that thickness."

Andre reached for a Magnum and happily fulfilled her request. He put the condom on and Aja quickly got on top of him riding him like a wild sexy beast. She tootsie rolled and butterflied all over his big dick. She was channeling Ciara, riding him to the beat of the song.

Andre couldn't take much more and exploded. He let out a loud moan and announced he was cumming. Aja smiled and felt like she put it down. Andre gave her a big kiss and said, "Girl why do you have to be married. Damn. If you were single I would tell you to start your firm here in NOLA."

She laughed and said, "I wish I met you sooner, ugh." They both looked deeply in each other's eyes and lay there enjoying each other's bodies over and over and over again. The sex they had that night was amazing.

It was about 5:00 a.m. when Aja's phone rang. Reality check—it was John. Oh no, she thought, what have I done? Aja jumped up and ran to the bathroom to take the call.

"Good morning, love. I'm headed to work and can't wait to see you baby. I hope you are behaving yourself. Don't forget you're a married woman."

Damn, why did he have to say that? Aja felt awful but played the good wife and told John she loved and missed him, too. She crept back into bed with Andre and stared at the ceiling before drifting back to sleep.

Aja was again jolted from deep slumber by her phone. This time it was Joann. She sounded as if she too had just awakened. Aja turned over and noticed Andre wasn't there. Her heart raced. She could hear Joann's voice, but she was in somewhat of a fog. Joann kept saying hello, but got no reply. Finally, Aja responded, and Joann said, "OK, girl. Meet me in the kitchen. The guys are cooking us breakfast." Aja brushed her teeth, staring at herself in the mirror in disbelief of what went down last night. She was full of mixed emotions. She gathered her thoughts grabbed the plush robe on the bed and headed downstairs. She saw Joann sitting at the island with a mimosa in hand. Joe was at the stove flipping pancakes, but Andre was nowhere to be seen. Aja asked, "Where is Dre? Um, I mean Andre?" Joe responded he had to leave for Miami this morning for a business meeting. Aja's heart sank. She felt like a fool. Oh, so you use me, fuck me good, get all you want and disappear, she thought. I knew it was too good to be true. She felt like a complete dummy for letting her guard down and being a total freak. It was good, but damn, he could have at least said something.

Joann noticed Aja was dazed and looking worried. She came over and asked if she was OK. Aja played it off and was like, yeah, of course. Joe was totally in his own world trying his hardest to impress the beautiful ladies he had in his presence with his culinary skills. "Breakfast is served, queens." They all ate and shared small talk. Noon rolled around and the girls began to panic. Their flight left at 3 that afternoon and they hadn't even been back to their hotels to pack. Joe and the ladies quickly dressed; he took the Bentley out to take them back to their hotels so they could get ready.

Aja was dropped off first. Joe and Joann said they would soon be back to get her so they could go to the airport together. As she dressed, Aja kept checking the phone thinking she would hear from Andre, but nothing. She cursed herself as she packed and prepared to head back home to her husband and secure life. Oh well, in the game sometimes you get played, she said to herself. Her emotions bubbled over and she burst into tears. Damn, she thought, the Bamma ain't sent flowers today like he did before he got this ass.

She was so upset; she had to get herself under control. She washed her face, put drops in her eyes and prepared to put on a good smile for Joann and Joe. They called and said they were at her hotel. Aja met them downstairs and they were off. She was quiet the whole ride to the airport. Joe and Joann laughed and entertained each other the entire time. Looks like they made a love connection, Aja said, jealously, under her breath.

"Southwest Air," Joe announced. "Here you ladies are. Wow, I enjoyed you guys these past couple of days. Joann, you know I'm coming to see you in DC in two weeks, baby."

The two of them had a long embrace. Aja was there all alone. Joe got their bags out and said, "Bye ladies. Oh, I almost forgot, Aja, my brother wanted me to give this card to you. He said don't open it until you land back home. He was sorry he had to leave so abruptly. He was feeling you, Shorty." Joe shook his head and kissed Joann on the forehead before leaving. Aja was totally in shock. She felt much better knowing Andre at least thought about her before leaving. Joe left and Joann said,

"Open it! Open it!"

"No, I'm going to wait. It has been a rough day, girl. I don't even want to talk about anything. Last night was what it was; I „took one for the team,' are you happy? Lets not discuss this, OK?"

Joann said, "So you got the start up funds?"

Aja shot her a look. And if looks could kill, Joann would be dead. Joann and Aja moved on to another subject but the discussion was dry. Joann was a little pissed by the way Aja was acting. She was happy when she heard the boarding announcement for the flight because it was sleepy time. She thought maybe a good rest would do Aja some good. Cranky ass. ...

Welcome to DCA. Wow, that flight was fast, Aja thought. She looked back and saw Joann, knocked out with her mouth wide open. She saw this as a perfect time to open the card. She did and out fell a check for $150,000. Aja smiled so big. She was on the way back to her old happy self. The check was nice but the note from Andre was even better. *"Hi beautiful. You are truly a queen. Last night was amazing; I want to thank you for sharing your precious time with me while you were in my city. I'm sorry I had to leave so quickly, I wanted to wake you but the way I was feeling you had me confused. I wanted to leave things as they were with the memory of no goodbyes, no feelings of regret or guilt. I told you I wanted to make your dreams come true so I wanted to bless you with this check. I hope this is enough to help you get your firm started, baby. Just know if your dude ever messes up I'm here for you, baby. Thinking of you always, Dre."*

Aja smiled and finally felt OK. She put the check in her wallet and but the card away as it was time to exit the plane.

Once at baggage claim Joann noticed a change in Aja's attitude and said, "Girl you seem much better. Are you ready to open that card?"

Aja smiled and answered, "Girl, are you ready to be partners with me in starting our new firm? Because I took one for the team and we are about to be bosses, baby."

The ladies laughed and headed towards the exit sign.

Today, Aja and Joann have their own firm and are preparing to hit next year's conference as owners of their business. It's also been said they visit New Orleans quite often—for investment meetings. ...

Nothing But the Butt

London was one of my most conservative clients (for the public). She stood five feet five with beautiful curly hair and caramel coated skin. She was a nurse by day and a freak by night. The stories she shared with me often made me want to lose my lunch. But just when I thought I heard it all, she dropped the bomb of all bombs on me—a dirty little secret about her man. ...

London and Lou seemed to be the perfect match. She was a nurse and he a physical therapist. They met on the job and instantly fell hard for one another. Lou was tall and dark, and while extremely overweight, he was well put together. He had style and always stayed fresh—he always wore the best clothes, shoes (he had every pair of Gucci and Prada sneakers) and just stayed *clean*. No, he wasn't the best looker but his swag was out of this world. His presence commanded attention. He drove a white Mercedes Benz S Class with all the bells and whistles.

People seeing him and London together would often comment on how well they complimented each other in every aspect of their relationship. Both were well educated, well traveled and came from great families. Lou adored the ground London walked on. She was equally in love with him, but to her girls she often complained about how unsatisfied she was in the bedroom. Remember, Lou was a big guy; *a really big guy*—standing six feet tall and he had to weigh well over 300 pounds. At one of London's lavish dinner parties her friends saw him wearing a Hermes belt and had to comment that they didn't know Hermes was made in his size. Of course, they assumed it couldn't be a knock-off 'cause they just knew everything about Lou was official.

Well, you know what they say about men who over compensate with their toys. And you also know what they say about big men—that they oftentimes have small packages. That was London's biggest complaint. She said Lou had the smallest penis she had ever seen (and felt, of course). She even said his balls were tiny and would sometimes disappear when he was excited. She would complain and complain about how she wished her "perfect man" had a bigger package so she could stop seeking pleasure outside their relationship. She felt bad about her secrets but just couldn't help herself—getting her freak on with Lou just wasn't happening. He didn't last long during sex and, strangely enough, always begged for London to put her fingers in his behind. London thought this was the nastiest thing ever and was turned off by his demands. But she loved her man. So she complied.

Each week London would faithfully come to my salon, sit in the chair and brag about a new sexual conquest—with a slew of random men. You see, London was a certified freak. She was thirty-eight and did not discriminate. You were fair game as long as you were over eighteen with a large penis. London believed in getting what she wanted, which was a big, fat, juicy dick. She would only accept nine inches or more.

London would roll up on guys she thought were nice looking and straight up ask how big their dick was because she was trying to fuck. No need to play games with this, what are you working with, she would say to them. Some of the guys were shocked and would walk away while others would be down and would whip their packages out on command. One guy named James allowed her to peep it and had her sprung.

London drove a white drop-top Lexus SC and first saw James when riding on Suitland Parkway. He was driving the same exact car as her. She pulled up beside James at a red light and their eyes locked. James gave her a huge smile, a perfectly white smile. He was a looker for sure. London's clit throbbed just thinking about how it would feel to be underneath this chocolate drop, feeling all of his chocolate thunder thrusting in and out of her. She snapped out of the zone as the cars behind her honked. She looked up and the light was green. James signaled her to pull over at the next light, which was the Naylor Road exit. London pulled over without hesitation.

They parked in the abandoned parking lot of the old Legend Nightclub. James hopped out his car and said, "Hello sunshine. You almost caused me an accident back there. What you doing driving by yourself? I think you need a partner in that passenger side. Can I get a ride?" London without hesitation said yes. She tried hard not to look thirsty but couldn't help herself. James had on a wife-beater, sweatpants and some Gucci flops. His muscles bulged out of the wife-beater. London looked down further and bam, jackpot. She saw the imprint from his juicy eggplant. London was already hot from the 90-degree DMV weather, but was on fire now that this chocolate God had a seat in her car. No sooner had James closed the door, London sped off. James was caught by surprise.

"Whoa, where are we going?"

"You said I needed a passenger for a ride and I couldn't agree with you more."

She pulled into a park around the corner from the Legend and leaned over to give her new friend a kiss. Not on the lips but down low.

James pushed London back and said, "Heyyyy, heyyy, I don't even know your name."

"London Jenkins. Let's get to all the petty stuff later. Right now I want to feel and taste your fat juicy cock."

James thought how crazy this was, but he leaned the seat back, looked around quickly, and then let London go to town. Her face lit up like a Christmas tree, as she was impressed by the length and width of his cock. She took his large eleven-inch chocolate dick deep into her throat and sucked his large penis like it was a chocolate Jell-O pudding pop. She licked around the perimeter of his large head and slurped making all types of sensual sounds. The head of his tool was smooth and looked to be the color of Dove's Dark chocolate. She could feel the vein underneath pulsating with each lick. James moaned and whispered, "Suck that dick like you need it." That drove London crazy she pulled her large Double-D breast out and massaged his dick with her boobs while she continued to give him oral pleasure.

She was excited that he didn't cum but also questioned her skills. She stopped for a moment and sat up. James turned to London and said, "Baby, why did you stop? Are you done? Please don't tell me you're done!" London didn't respond. She was stuck thinking about how she used all of her tricks on James, which normally would have made any of her boy-toys explode. Before she could question her skills further, James reached down and rubbed on her clit in a circular motion. London quickly glided his hand down to where her juices flowed, giving him an invitation for more. He leaned in and took one of her plump breasts in his mouth and began to suckle like she was about to quench his thirst with some breast milk. London moaned in ecstasy and opened her legs so James could get an even better feel. James whispered in her ear, asking, "Are you ready?"

London being the type of woman she was asked, "Am I ready for what?" She wanted to hear what exactly he was asking her, *what she was ready for*.

James smiled bashfully and said, "You know. Are you ready?"

London looked down at his rock-hard dick and grabbed it. She replied with a smile and said, "What do you think I drove over here for. Certainly not for bird watching."

James looked around to make sure no one was in the area. He took a condom out of his pocket and wrapped his large chocolate bar for protection. London climbed on top, lifted her white sundress up and proceeded to ride him like she was at a Texas rodeo. Her nipples were stiff from excitement and her large breasts slapped James in the face as she moved her body up and down. James grabbed her ass and grinded and pumped back with every motion. The moment was full of lust. The heat from both of their hot bodies was electric and could have jumpstarted a car. The wetness of her pleasure box soaked his large tool. All you could hear were the seductive sounds of sex.

London whimpered in James' ear as he went deeper and deeper inside. "Is this pussy good to you?" London asked.

At that moment James let out a big moan. London then said, "Cum for me baby." She wasn't about to tell him, but her legs were hurting from riding him for so long. Just as if cued to cum, James blurted out, "I'm cumming, baby. I'm cumming."

He and London stopped, looked at each other and burst into laughter. London slid off of James' lap and pulled her dress down. James fixed his clothing and threw the condom out the window.

London just sat in the driver's seat and stared at this fine chocolate man, wondering when she could get round two. James and London sat in the parking lot for about an hour talking about each other's situations, lives and interests. Families were starting to head over to the playground so London used that as her excuse to roll out. She got what she wanted and knew Lou would be home waiting for dinner. She looked at her dashboard clock and said, "I really need to get going. Let's exchange numbers and plan to do this again, same time same place tomorrow."

James shook his head and said, "No need for us to do it here. I live up the street in the Carriage Hill apartments. Meet me tomorrow, same time, my place."

London agreed and took James back to his car. They kissed, said their good byes and drove off.

London rode home happy as can be. She had the top down as DJ Khaled's "Hold You Down" played in the background and all she could think about was the latest sexy addition to her sex boy-toy line up. London was one to hump and run, but sometimes she kept her toys and put them in heavy rotation. She considered James rotation worthy.

London turned the radio down as she entered her exclusive Woodmore neighborhood, which was one of the most prestigious communities in Prince Georges County. As expected, Lou's car was in the garage. As soon as she hit the front door, he yelled out what's for dinner? London rolled her eyes and ignored his inquiry. She ran up the stairs to the master bedroom to undress and hit the shower. She heard Lou coming up the stairs after her, moving quickly as if Michael Myers was chasing him. She twisted her face up like to say, why is Big Lou running? He rushed into the bedroom with an urgent look. Out of breath and sweating bullets, Lou asked, "Have you been in the bathroom yet?"

London shook her head and said, "No, why?"

"Oh, OK," Lou said. "Don't go in the bathroom yet. I have a surprise."

London was no dumb girl and was on his heels as he walked to the bathroom. She was floored by what she saw. There were two yellow anal plugs and they were not in a box. They were out on the corner of her tub sitting on her favorite zebra print towel. Lou tried to grab them up quickly but it was too late. London had already seen what made her man act all weird. She slapped the plugs out of his hand and screamed, "Louis Brown what do you have those anal plugs for?"

Lou looked like a dear in the headlights. He was totally caught off guard and couldn't believe London went straight upstairs before he had a chance to hide "her surprise." He quickly responded, "Baby, I wanted us to try something different tonight. I was told that a man can have a very intense organism with anal pressure, you know like how I enjoy having you put your finger in my? …"

"Ughhhh!" London interrupted. "I don't want to hear it. You want to do what? So why are there two?"

"You see, there are two anal plugs for a reason," Lou said, explaining he got one for her as well. He wanted them both to use the plugs, together. London felt slightly relieved. Although Lou didn't please her sexually, she loved her man. She shook the crazy thoughts swirling in her head and said, "OK baby, we can play tonight. But first let momma take a bath."

Lou said hold up what about my dinner? London gave him the side eye and said, "You better warm up some beans and franks."

Lou said he would cook only if she promised to try the plugs tonight. London said cool and proceeded to run her bath water.

After dinner London went upstairs hoping she could get out of her promise to Lou. Big Lou was on the couch eating chips and playing Madden with his brother. She just knew she had escaped and she laid in their king-size bed watching "Love and Hip Hop New York." Just as she was yelling at the TV during one of Erica and Chrissy's fights, Lou strolled in the room in his birthday suit. London rolled her eyes. She truly was not in the mood to have any anal plug in her ass, nor was she in the mood to use it on Lou. London tried to act like she was tired and let out a big yawn. Lou said, "Naw baby, you can't try that tired mess with me tonight. I just heard you yelling at your TV show. Plus, a promise is a promise. Come on do something to make Big Daddy feel good."

London could see how excited Lou was. So she got herself together, began to undress and stood up face to face with Lou. She reached down and gave a playful tug to his manhood—his two inches quickly grew to three. London loved how powerful she felt being with such a large man. When London got a hold of Lou he was like putty in her hands, literally. She loved how soft his belly and body felt pressed against her frame. London was now in the mood, from kissing and rubbing Lou's large body. She pushed him back on the bed and continued deeply kissing her man. Lou stopped the tongue action and paused to say, "Baby, I saw your facial expression earlier when I had the plugs. But just know I want to try all my fantasies with you."

Lou set the mood by lighting some candles and putting on their favorite sexing Pandora station, R. Kelly. The sounds of R. Kelly's "Strip for You" came across the speakers as things were heating up. Lou went into the drawer of his cherry wood nightstand and pulled out some wet anal lubrication and the anal plugs. He instructed London to lay back and relax. London closed her eyes and tried to relax as much as she could. Lou kissed London's neck then he began to gently caress her breasts. He then moved down to her perfectly manicured pussy and began to lick and suck all of her juices. He pushed her legs back as far as they could go, having her feet meet her head. London knew when Lou put her in the Cirque du Soleil position he was about to handle his business. He used his tongue to tease and please London. He knew all of London's spots and twirled his tongue in the exact zone to make her crazy. He licked London like a professional, slid his chubby fingers deep into her pussy and sucked on her clit until she exploded. There was a small puddle from the drip drops of her juices. London was in the zone and didn't want him to stop. One thing about Lou—although he couldn't please her with his manhood, his oral technique deserved an award. Lou instructed London to bend over. Feeling like a million bucks she complied, what came next she was not expecting.

Lou typically would eat London, then bend her over and enter her from behind for his two-minute pump. But Lou had different plans tonight. He bent her over and splat the lubrication on her anal entrance. He then proceeded to insert the anal plug. London was uncomfortable and extremely tense, so the plug wouldn't go in. Lou instructed her to relax and he tried repeatedly to insert the plug. He said, "OK, I guess you aren't ready yet. But," he asked, "are you ready to try it on me?" Then he added, "But, London, please promise not to tell anyone." London promised and without her direction Lou bent over and took that anal plug like a pro.

The plug was yellow, fat and about three inches in depth. London was shocked at how easy the plug slid in. Lou squealed, "Yes, London, yes. You are the best girlfriend a man could ever have." London was frozen. She had done a lot in her thirty-eight years, but nothing like this. Lou said, "OK, baby, now lick my balls!" London wanted to scream what balls? His balls did a disappearing act, as usual. London didn't want to seem rude or show her disgust, so she just licked the area where his sack would normally be. Lou reached his hand around to his backside and played with the plug as London licked and played with his penis. Lou moaned from the pleasure he was receiving and whispered, "Baby, now I want to feel you." Without instruction, London got on all fours arching her back just how Lou liked it. He slid inside her warm wet walls and slowly thrust in and out of her wetness. London's round ass shook with each thrust. This turned Lou on; he loved seeing her ass wiggle when he had her from behind. Not even four minutes in, Lou exploded from the pleasure he received. He got up and walked into the bathroom locking the door. London just laid in bed thinking, what the hell just happened?

The morning sun shined brightly in London's eyes as she laid solo in the bed. Smells of bacon flooded the house. This quickly woke London out of her morning fog. She threw her leopard print robe on and walked downstairs. Lou was at the stove in the kitchen listening to 92.3, enjoying the Rickey Smiley morning show. He was laughing at the prank phone call that was on, totally unaware that his lady was sitting behind him. He turned around startled to see London at the table. He greeted his boo with a kiss and said, "You ruined my surprise, love. I was planning to serve you breakfast in bed to show you how much I appreciate what you did for me last night." He had a dozen red long stem roses and a bottle of Moët on the large granite island. He walked to the table and presented them to her with a wide smile. London said, "Wow baby. You are just full of surprises lately." Lou didn't know how to take her remark and was about to say something about it but decided to just let it go. He finished making their five-star meal of crab-cake Eggs Benedict, crab hash, Canadian bacon and Belgium waffles with a lemon truffle filling. They toasted to their love while sipping Moet mimosas.

Eight a.m. rolled around and it was time for Lou to head off to work. London had the next three days off. Being a registered nurse really had its perks and she saw this time as her opportunity to get into mischief. She sent James a text as soon as Lou's Benz hit the corner to exit their block. "Hey, chocolate. You ready for round two? XOXO." London smiled and thought, yes, this text should surely get James' attention. Ten o'clock rolled around. Eleven. Then noon. Nothing from James. The afternoon flew past and London was getting heated. It was 4:30 p.m. and still no response from James. London being the spoiled princess she was, deleted his number and started preparing dinner for Lou.

Lou came home and walked through the door with a large Gucci bag. He called London to take a look at the surprise he had for her this evening. He jokingly said, "Yeah, you said I was full of surprises lately so I figured, why stop? Take a look inside, babe."

London peaked in the bag and to her pleasant surprise there was the red, large leather Gucci Soho handbag that she had been saving for the past three months. London was too thrilled; she pranced around modeling her latest gift. She was all smiles until she looked inside it (as it felt a little heavy) and found a larger-sized anal plug. Her stomach sank and her mouth watered as if she had to vomit. She gained her composure and said, "What is this," pointing inside the bag.

"Baby, tonight I want to try to push my limits. You mind easing this in me."

London couldn't help but be transparent and asked, "Where is all this anal exploration coming from?"

Lou explained that he overheard some of the guys at the gym talking about anal plugs and how intense the release was when they used the plugs during sexual acts. He decided he wanted to try them with her. London took a deep breath in and thought to herself, hell if I won't do it, someone else will. She knew what she was doing to get pleased outside of her relationship and couldn't bear to think of her Louie panting with somebody else. London stripped nude in the foyer for Lou and put that Gucci bag on her shoulder, heading in the direction of the kitchen.

She turned and signaled Lou to follow her. She pulled her big bear in close and tongued him down. While kissing him, she unbuttoned his pants and whispered, "drop them." Lou was too happy to comply. She then said, "Baby, take care of me. I want to fill you inside of me." Lou said OK, and bent London over as usual and he entered her gently and pumped maybe six times before cumming. He pulled out and looked at London's shapely body like she was on the menu. London loved seeing how her man admired her, so she decided to just go for what Lou desired. She said, "Bend over baby. Let mommy take care of you." She then pulled the plug out of the bag and entered Lou with it, repeating what took place the night before. She licked his missing sack and sucked his penis, while he played with his ass using the plug. Lou groaned and came all over the kitchen floor. Lou was embarrassed with how loud he was and how he seemed to really get off from the plug more than from having traditional sex with London.

This routine of the anal plug lasted for days. Soon Lou was refusing to have intercourse with London; he just wanted the plug action. This new situation with Lou wasn't sitting well with her. She was also feeling down because she hadn't heard from James. He was supposed to be on her rotation team. Things were just not going her way.

London decided to call her girlfriend Freda for drinks. The two divas met at Grace's at the National Harbor and as she walked up the stairs to the main dining area who does London see but Mr. "missing in action" James. He was sitting at the table with a cute Brad Pitt-looking dude. The two handsome-looking men appeared to be deep in conversation. The server escorted the ladies to their table. London desperately wanted to walk over to say something to him, but she kept cool and took her seat. Freda was spilling her heart out to London about the fight she had last night with her baby daddy, Troy, but blah, blah, blah was all London heard. She had completely zoned out thinking about James, and if, when, and how she should make her presence known to him.

Just when she had plotted things out, she made a quick change in plans when she saw James walk towards the bathroom. Being the wild and spontaneous woman she was, she decided to surprise her missing lover in his most vulnerable moment—inside the men's bathroom. She quickly cut Freda off in her rundown of how Troy went through her phone and found a suspicious text. London excused herself, and the walk to the bathroom seemed like the longest walk ever. Outside the men's room, she hesitated for a quick second, looked around the hallway and then pushed through the door. She walked in and luckily there was no one else in the restroom besides her and James. His back was turned to the door as he was using the urinal. The clicking of her six-inch Christian Louboutins didn't belong in the men's restroom.

James jerked his neck around to see who entered his space. To his surprise it was London. He was in total shock and said, "Hey, you don't belong in here. You better get out before someone sees you."

London replied in a smart tone, "Let them, I don't give a damn. You know I love putting on shows." She walked up on him from behind pressing her body on his back. She whispered in his ear, while grabbing his crotch, "How dare you take my chocolate away from me."

James didn't know what to do. He was totally caught off guard, but unable to control nature, his hefty flesh tower grew and stiffened instantly. He turned around to face London and before he could get a word out, she shoved her tongue down his throat. The sight of James made London forget that this man had disappeared on her, ignored her texts, and disappointed her deeply. Their embrace and kisses were intense. James pushed London towards the sink and picked her up while lifting her sundress in one movement. London was commando and James took full advantage, sliding his manhood in her wet box. In fact, her pussy was so wet he slid in with ease as she moaned, "Oh fuck, oh fuck," as his pleasure rod took her to another dimension of satisfaction. London moaned as he rhythmically slid in and out of her. He went slow and deep, at the same time whispering naughty things in London's ear. She cupped his ass, pulling him deeper and deeper inside. While in sexual bliss, they missed the sound of footsteps approaching the door. It was James' handsome friend entering the bathroom. James' friend gasped as he saw the two wild lovers in the animalistic sex act. Then he said in a very soft tone, "Oh wow, you get down like that J? I'm so over this." He angrily walked off. James snapped out of the sexual spell he was under, pulled out of London and quickly got his pants up, zipped and ran after his friend.

Once again, London felt used and worthless. She couldn't even imagine how angry Freda was. She was ashamed but got herself together and walked back to her table. Freda looked extremely pissed. She had a drink in her hand and rolled her eyes as London approached the table. When London sat down the waitress came to the table and said, "Oh, you are the other half of the party. Your friend has already ordered her food what would you like?" London was so disturbed about what just happened with James that she was in a daze and couldn't respond. This made Freda even more upset. She told the waitress, "Put my order in a box to go. I don't think my friend wants to be here." London burst into tears as the waitress stood there with a look on her face like what is going on tonight? First, the fine Brad Pitt-looking dude left here in tears, and now you…

The beautiful blonde waitress shook her head and told Freda, "I„ll be back with your food boxed and your check, no rush." Freda quickly got up and sat on the same side of the booth as London giving her good friend a tight hug. She asked, "What's going on with you girl?" London was silent, still hurt and in tears. Freda repeated herself, this time in a stern tone, "What the heck is going on with you? You been on Mars all night. You left me for 30 minutes. You were clearly not in the ladies room as you said. What the hell is going on?"

London stuttered, "I ran off because, because…hmmm, I saw that guy, James, here. I told you about him. I went to confront him and lost it."

"Oh, you lost it. I know what that means," Freda said. "You went animal planet on him didn't you? So, where is this James now, and why are you crying?" Freda asked.

London shrugged her shoulders and continued crying frantically. The waitress came back with the box and check. Freda paid the bill and kept comforting London as best she could. London then began telling Freda everything, and they had a big cry together. Freda told London she needed to let that situation go, as it appeared London caught feelings and James clearly doesn't feel the same. "Sounds like you're sprung. But you have a good man at home. You need to stop being in these streets sleeping with different men," Freda said with genuine concern. "You know there are all types of STDs out here and crazies. Shoot I watch the ID network and freak-out thinking of these creeps. Just chill and go home to Lou. That man loves you."

London listened and thanked her friend for forgiving her selfish actions that evening. The ladies continued sitting at Grace's and ordered appetizers and drinks. Soon the mood changed from tense to festive, as Freda changed the subject to reality television, chatting and laughing about the latest episodes of "Love and Hip Hop," "The Real Housewives of Atlanta" and "Tamar and Vince." The evening came to a pleasant close for the two friends, and they each went their separate ways.

The ride home for London was long and dark, as she kept replaying what took place at the restaurant in her head. How could I be so stupid, she thought. I need to seriously get a grip on reality. Just when she felt the tears about to flow, her phone rang and it was James. London picked up the call on her car's Bluetooth system. James said, "Hello beautiful. I just wanted to apologize for leaving the way I did. I was tied up in a business meeting and when I saw you, I had to have it. You know you got that good, good. The investor I was meeting with caught us in the bathroom. I had to rush out. I really and truly apologize."

London didn't respond, there was just silence on her end. She wanted to believe James, but was just tired of being disappointed. Surprised by how London was non-responsive, James continued, "Hey, beautiful—you still there?" London in a very low tone responded, yes. James pleaded for her forgiveness and asked for her to meet him at his place in an hour. London hesitated. But the lust in her for James was stronger than her pride and dignity. She agreed to meet him in an hour. She stopped past her house to freshen up and to let Lou know she and Freda were going to the Look Lounge for the rest of the evening. She had to come up with something or Lou would be suspicious.

London pulled up to her beautiful home, but to her pleasant surprise Lou wasn't there. She quickly showered and dressed so she could continue her sexcapade with James. She called Lou twice from their home phone before leaving the house and left a voicemail message letting her other half know she would be gone for the rest of the night. London was a little pissed she couldn't get Lou on the phone, but the feeling of anger quickly left with thoughts of James having his way with her played in her mind. London jumped in her Lexus and speed off into the night.

As London entered James' complex she saw a Benz that looked just like Lou's exiting. London was a bit nervous since James did not live in the best of neighborhoods. It wasn't an everyday thing to see cars like that in his parking lot. London shook it off and parked her car behind James' building instead of in front in an effort to conceal her presence.

James beat London to the door as he heard the clicking of her Emily B heels approaching. James greeted her in his birthday suit. He was completely nude and smelling fresh as if he just jumped out of the shower. He greeted London with a sloppy kiss on the lips and pulled her into his cozy apartment. James wasted no time getting down to business. They kissed and kissed, and he soon was lifting London's dress over her curvy figure. He threw her on the bed, pulled her sheer panties down with his teeth and threw her legs back so he could get full access. He dove right in and parted the lips of her juice box with his fingers and began licking her pink flesh. As he felt her body shake, he flicked his tongue faster and faster along the side of her pussy lips.

He stopped and told London he wanted them to cum together. He laid back and placed her on his face in the reverse cowgirl position so they could pleasure each other at the same time. James made his tongue stiff and stuck it inside London's sugar walls. She took him in her warm mouth and juiced his hard rod up so well it felt like her mouth was a pussy. There was a lot of moaning from both of them. James felt himself about to cum so he sucked on her clit and flicked his tongue faster hoping they would climax together and they did. It was like an atomic bomb. James' toes curled as he shot his load into her mouth and he stuffed his face deep into her wetness and exhaled. They were dripping wet from their foreplay session and took a shower together. That made things even steamier.

Fresh out the shower, James rubbed hot oils all over London's body. The smell of Lilac and Jasmine soon filled the room. He started with her shoulders, and sensual thoughts ran through London's head. She moaned as James worked his way down from her back to her plump round ass. But then she felt something slippery around the entrance of her anus. It felt familiar like some sort of lubricant. James continued to massage London's caramel glazed body then he stopped and instructed her to bend that ass over. London got into the doggy-style position and James whispered in a sensual tone, "I want to try something different."

London thought to herself, first Lou, now James, what's going on with the men in my life? James asked have you tried anal plugs before? London hesitated in answering the question, but said to herself, girl just be honest. Yes, she replied.

"Really?" he said. "Oh, well, I won't start you off with the beginner plug. I have a little larger one. London couldn't believe what she was hearing, what's up with the fascination with anal plugs lately? Her mind was wondering, and then suddenly, she felt this immense pressure from James inserting the anal plug. He asked her if she was OK, as he continued to massage her body with oils. London was not ready for the larger size plug and was quite uncomfortable. But she was too embarrassed to say anything and because she didn't want to mess up and end up losing touch with James, London went along with him. James palmed and squeezed London's cheeks and slowly poured some warm oil down her crack. He then entered London from behind, grinding his long stick inside her sugar walls. James slid his fingers down to her clit and rubbed her pussy. London was in pure amazement in how incredible things felt with the pressure of having both of her holes filled. Her large tits bounced from side to side as he shoved it in and out, deeper and deeper. She shivered in pleasure as his balls slapped against her as he pounded her pussy mercilessly. James' warm breath was heavy on her neck and he moaned as his body shook from having an intense orgasm. He slid out of London and said, "Baby, you are so pretty, you are so pretty. I hope I just got back in your good graces." London threw a pillow at him and smiled. All the hurt feelings from earlier had vanished. She got her "happy" back. London lay in James' king-size bed and drifted off to sleep.

DJ Khaled's song, "I Wanna Be With You," rang across London's phone at 4:00 a.m. This was Lou's ring tone but London was sleeping like a baby. James looked at the phone and saw her man was the caller. He rolled his eyes and pushed the reject call button sending Lou's call straight to voicemail. The phone rang again, this time James turned her phone on silent. He knew he was wrong but was feeling vicious and in control. He had plans for London. James sat there and gently rubbed London's body as she slept the night away. He just couldn't take his eyes off of her as he admired her beauty.

The sunrays peeped through James' window shades and London woke to the beams of light in a panic. She quickly grabbed her phone to look at the time, 7:45 a.m. As she did, she also saw twelve missed calls from Lou. "Oh shit!!!!" she yelled. "How the hell did I sleep through twelve freaking calls?" She looked at her phone and saw her ringer had been switched to silent. Her heart dropped and felt like it was in her stomach.

"What the, how the? Oh my, my, this muthafucka..." she couldn't get the words out. She was full of anger and shook James. In a state of rage, she yelled, "I know you turned my ringer off you jerk. How could you?"

James responded instantly, as if he wasn't really asleep, and had this devilish look on his face. He said, " I just did what needed to be done. You take Big Lou for granted."

London's jaw dropped. "How exactly do you know my man's name?"

"No, you mean ,,our man,' honey." London could not believe her ears as James continued, "Yes, you think we met by chance? Well, we sort of did. But you played right into my plan to break you and Lou up. Lou is one of my biggest clients and I just couldn't have you messing my cash flow up. You see I'm the CEO of Discrete LLC. I own a discrete male escort business and Lou pays top dollar for this chocolate."

London lost control of her bodily fluids and passed out from the news she just received. James got scared. He didn't know if he had killed London with the news. He was nervous but quickly calmed down once London came to. He grabbed a bottle of water and gave it to her. She refused to take the water and said, "I'm out of here. I don't believe anything you have to say."

James stopped her and said, "Well, before you leave let me show you something. Matter of fact you aren't going anywhere until you watch this short independent film I have. See I was afraid you would say you didn't believe me, so I've got a little insurance. Just sit back and watch. I'll even pop some popcorn for you boo."

London was afraid of what was about to be shown on the fifty-inch flat screen but she knew she had to sit there and watch in order to know for sure if what James was saying was true. "The first clip was from last night," James said. "Lou came through to drop off a check in an effort to calm me down after I threatened to tell you his dirty little secret."

Sure enough, in the video clip Lou entered James' apartment and handed him an envelope. "He told me he no longer needed my services and that he was trying to get his life in order to live a normal life with you. He also told me that you accepted him and his ass fetish with butt plugs. He wanted you both to go to counseling after he found condoms in your shoeboxes. He said you two don't use condoms. Next time you got to be more careful honey."

James grabbed London's face and smiled to let her know he meant business.

London spit on James and said, "So what! This clip just shows him walking in giving you the check and you crying like a little bitch."

James was heated by her response and actions, but just laughed and rewound the video to a clip of him plowing Lou from behind. "Oh, look how *your man cries like a bitch*, for my dick, that is."

London couldn't believe her eyes. She begged James to stop the video. James ignored her request and rewound the video back to other clips of him and Lou in their sex sessions. One scene even had the white gentleman she saw James with at Grace's. Lou and James had the other guy in the Eiffel Tower position. London was beyond disgusted.

Full of tears she could barely talk, but found the strength enough to scream, "OK, OK, I get it. My man has a secret life. Are you happy? You got what you wanted, I'm done."

James laughed and said, "See you whore. You aren't the only one with dirty little secrets."

Two the Hard Way

Let me introduce you to Amy Clark, my Caucasian sister with a black-girl booty. I had the pleasure of styling Amy when I worked as a freelance stylist in LA for a couple of years in the late '90s. Amy had some truly amazing stories that made me want to shadow her for a day or two. She was a woman who knew what she wanted and always found a way to get it. She recently came to DC on business and called me to meet her for drinks at the W Hotel. This is one of the stories she told me that had me a little jealous. Check it out and see why...

It was another hot summer day in Southern California. Amy Clark lay in the beaming sun trying desperately to maintain her perfectly bronzed skin. Amy was a looker for sure. She stood five foot eight, with a curvaceous body and legs for days. Her long, silky strawberry blonde hair with platinum highlights always made people wonder if blondes really had more fun. But her breasts were what she used to hypnotize the many men that crossed her path. Her eyes were a shade of cerulean blue and were equally hypnotizing. Amy had a way of attracting very successful men from all types of backgrounds. She had dated NBA players to successful CEOs of Fortune 500 companies. The girl seemed to have all the luck with men.

One Friday afternoon Amy decided to play hooky from the office. She was feeling a little stressed and needed a break. Little did she know her decision to ditch work would land her into the adventure of her life. Amy was sunbathing when this tall sexy hot-bodied guy approached her interrupting her me time. He tapped her on the leg and asked could he join her. Slightly irritated, Amy pulled her Chanel shades off to get a better look at this guy who disturbed her daydream. This was the guy she spotted earlier while pulling into the beach parking lot. Sometimes people appear attractive until you get a closer look; to her surprise her eyes were not playing tricks on her. Standing in front of her was perfection in the male form. Amy quickly said to him, "And you are?"

He gave out a laugh and in an Italian accent said, "Amadeo."

Amy licked her lips then repeated, "Amadeo. Hmmm, that's a sexy name."

Amadeo blushed and said, "Why thank you. You're a sexy woman. And what might this sexy woman's name be?"

Amy giggled and said, "Nothing exotic, just plain old Amy."

"Well it's nothing plain about Amy," he said. "You are one beautiful work of art."

"Thanks. You tapped me for a reason?" Amy asked. "What's up, Mr. Amadeo?"

"You. I'd love to lay with you and get to know you a little better," Amadeo said.

Amy and Amadeo spent the rest of their day together on the beautiful sands of Manhattan Beach and had dinner at a quaint outdoor restaurant, Rock'N Fish, just steps from the beach. They enjoyed each other with plenty of drinks and laughs. The chemistry between the two was definitely there and they both knew they wanted to see each other again. Amadeo asked for Amy's number, and gave her his as well. They both agreed to set up an official date for the following night, which was on a Saturday.

Amy rushed home and called her best friend Kayla to tell her about her encounter with this exotic, buff guy. Kayla answered in her thick Dominican accent in a very irritated tone. "Amy you should know not to call me when „Tiny and Shekinah' are on! This is a NO CALL zone!" Amy begged for her girl's forgiveness and explained her reason for disrupting her TV time. Kayla quickly pushed pause on her remote when she heard the excitement in Amy's voice. As Amy shared her story, Kayla grew equally excited for her bestie and suggested they go shopping in the morning to get a new sexy outfit for her hot date. Amy hung up the phone with Kayla and lay in her bed, thinking about Amadeo and how good he would feel kissing, rubbing and caressing her body. She became so turned on by her naughty thoughts she took out her bullet. It was a while since she touched herself and her body was aching for some pleasure. She pulled up her favorite porn site Hamster.com and rubbed her clit with the bullet in a slow pulsating rhythm. She intensely watched the lovers on the screen and fantasized about that being she and Amadeo. She teased her clit, pretending it was Amadeo's stiff tongue. "Ohhhh, Ummm," she moaned aloud, until she had an explosive orgasm. It was sweet dreams after that.

Saturday morning arrived and Amy met Kayla at her home. It was another beautiful day in sunny California, so the girls put the windows down and opened the sunroof as they climbed into Amy's all white Range Rover. The sun was shining on their glistening skin, the wind breezed in their shiny hair, and the girls were really feeling themselves as they cruised to South Bay Galleria mall.

Once there, they walked around enjoying the boutiques and shops, seeing a few possible choices and buying their top picks. A few hours passed, the friends were getting hungry, and decided to head out with what they already purchased. On their way to the parking lot, Amy got the heel of one of her Versace shoes stuck into a crack in the floor and tripped, almost falling. A man walking past caught her in his robust arms, held her tightly and helped her to safety. He asked, "Are you OK? You almost hit the floor! I'm glad I was walking by when I was. Guess it was meant for me to save you."

Amy's face turned red from embarrassment but she was smooth in how she played it off. "Thank you so much! I'm OK, especially now since you came to my rescue. My hero! What's your name, Superman?"

"Giovanni," he answered. "What's your name, beautiful?"

She blushed and said, "Amy, and this is my bestie, Kayla." They all said nice to meet you and Giovanni wasted no time asking for Amy's number. They exchanged numbers and Giovanni told Amy that he'd be in touch soon so they can set a date to link up for dinner. Amy agreed. The girls walked out into the parking lot, as Giovanni walked into the mall.

Kayla said to Amy, "Girl you are on a roll! Two hot guys in two days! Damn, I'm getting a little jealous! Can I at least get one? Whichever one you like the least. I'll take a pass over, not a hand me down! So please pass one of those fine men over here." They laughed hysterically.

"Girl, you are crazy! Oh, my gosh, I can't take you right now, Girl!" Amy replied, barely getting the words out while laughing so hard. They were still laughing as they packed their shopping bags into the trunk of the truck.

Kayla said excitedly, "I'm sorry girl but he was gorgeous! He might end up your husband one day, so forgive me. But his dark blue eyes had me. Then his beautiful dark hair and beard, oh and his smooth olive skin, And damn, his smile, and I can't forget to mention his bangin' body! That was the closest I've seen of a guy I would sleep with on the spot! Girl he can get it!"

Amy agreed and they had some more laughs as they got back to discussing the best choice for her outfit for the night. Their light conversation continued as they enjoyed lunch at Little Sister, their favorite local spot. About an hour later, Amy dropped Kayla off, and headed home to get some rest before she had to get ready for her big date.

It wasn't long before it was time for her to decide what to wear. She hopped out of a hot, steamy shower, put on her silk robe, and rubbed her body down with lotion. She decided to go with the one-piece navy blue and black color block jumpsuit that hugged her natural curves just right, and featured a low plunging neckline that showed just enough cleavage to have eyes popping and mouths drooling. She stepped into her Navy blue YSL stilettos and finished putting up her hair in a sexy messy pin up. Yes, she was looking photo-shoot ready.

She met Amadeo at this Asian cuisine restaurant called Hakkasan Beverly Hills. She met him there because she didn't let guys know where she lived until she was comfortable with them. That is if they even stayed in the game long enough. Amy arrived and valet parked her car, she walked in and everyone noticed. She told the hostess the name of her date and the thin dark-haired hostess sent a waiter over to escort her to her table. Amadeo was waiting with a beautiful bouquet of long-stem red roses and a smile. Amy saw him and got excited. She was thinking to herself, wow, he's so sexy, look at that face with those dimples, and he bought flowers. If he keeps adding up the brownie points, he might get invited for a nightcap. Momma, be a lady, now. Stay classy, lol. And she did.

Amadeo saw her coming towards him and he similarly was aroused. He was truly astonished by her beauty. She was very polished; attractive from her head to her toes. Oh, he thought, she is a Goddess. Amadeo stood to seat her, and handed her the bouquet of flowers he brought. She flashed a brilliant smile and thanked him. They took to ordering drinks and appetizers, and then their entrees, while they indulged in great conversation. The atmosphere and food was amazing. Amy couldn't get over how good the Curried Sea Bass was. They were both enjoying the food, but enjoyed each other's company even more as they flirted, and admired each other's sex appeal and attractiveness. Amadeo started to sweat, as he couldn't stop glancing at Amy's plump bosom. He was happy he was seated as the heat-seeking missile between his legs started to twitch and lift off its launching pad.

Amy was one to typically take things slow, but she was really feeling Amadeo. So as their dinner neared its end, she decided to extend the date by inviting him to her condo for coffee and pie.

Amadeo laughed and said, "Pie? I would love to stick my finger in that warm delicious-looking pie, and then lick it. I love tasting pretty pies!"

Amy acted like she wasn't interested in that type of action for the night, but her pussycat was throbbing and purring under the table as they spoke. She told him to be on his best behavior and he might be able to check out her "pie." They both laughed and headed out. Once the valet brought their cars, Amadeo followed Amy to her place. They entered her condo and she showed him around. Amy had done extremely well for herself and was proud of it. Her home was two levels, with a luxurious rooftop patio and an amazing skyline view. The Jacuzzi tub and stone fire pit made her rooftop appealing. Her hardwood floors, contemporary décor and stainless steel appliances made her place look like something out of the pages of Elle Décor magazine.

They walked into her spacious bedroom and Amy kicked off her shoes and told him that he's special because she never brought anyone to her place on the first date, but she is really feeling him and liked his vibe. Amdaeo blushed and whispered in her ear, licking it just barely, "I want some of that warm, sweet pie." He added, softly, "Emmm, can I see it? I just wanna taste it! If that's all you want me to do, I'm fine with that. Just let me put my tongue in it and taste it!"

He kissed her neck and down to her breast, dropping the top of her jumpsuit to her waist. He played with her enormous boobs, licking them wildly with his tongue out, moving his head from side to side. Then he kissed her stomach and dropped the bottom half of her jumpsuit to the floor. He saw her sexy red lace panties then pulled them off! Amadeo was super turned on and told her how pretty her kitty was. His mouth watered while he asked her in a moaning sexy voice, "Can I kiss her, and make her mine for tonight?"

Amy moaned, "Yes, please, she can be yours for tonight!"

He started teasing her clit with his mouth, sliding his thick wet tongue across her entrance and then back to her pink love button. He paused for a moment and then went back to his playful tease. He enjoyed the sounds Amy made when he paid special attention to her clit. He repeated this routine several times. Satisfied by the sweet creamy presence from Amy's box and sensual whimpers of pleasure, Amdaeo decided it was the right time to dive in. He started passionately kissing her kitty and sucking on her clit, making her moan and tell him how good it felt. Goose bumps formed with each lick. He quickly picked her up noticing her hard nipples, he caressed each breast and showed each of them precise attention. Licking and teasing her nipples with his tongue, he laid her on the bed then went back to French kissing that kitty until it purred. Amy's body jerked as she came on his lips and tongue while he continued to kiss and lick her pussy. Amadeo's mouth and chin were shiny and wet from the flood of pleasure juice Amy released. Satisfied, she told him to take down his pants and without hesitation, Amadeo took off his clothes. He was butt naked in a matter of seconds. Amy kissed him and rubbed her fingers through his thick black hair, then grabbed his back with both hands and massaged him while kissing him passionately. She then pushed him on the bed to let him know she meant business.

Amy got on her knees, and thought it would be a good idea to tease Amadeo too. She kissed his thighs slowly and wrapped both of her hands around his hard, throbbing cock. She jerked his tool, while licking his balls. He let out a loud moan as she playfully licked the shaft of his penis. She paused and caressed his thighs, kissing them gently. Amadeo's breathing changed as she licked his love sack and put them in her mouth. Amy jerked his cock while heating up his balls with her warm wet mouth. He looked down at her and said, "Damn Amy, that feels good, go ahead and give him a kiss. Stop playing."

Amy smiled and said, "Oh, it's ok for you to play, but not me? Be patient, I want to give him a kiss. Believe me, just lay back and be patient. Her tease continued as she licked the base of his hard stick slowly, licking up and down as if his cock was an ice cream cone. Sensing that her new lover was craving more, she ended the torturous tease and placed his thick juicy stick in her mouth, slowly going all the way down on it until she could feel it in her throat. She sucked on it sloppily like a porn star, jerking it and spitting on it, then sucking it some more. While her mouth was juicy and slippery, she rubbed some of the natural juices on his balls and rubbed it into them while continuing to go up, down, and around on him. She made loud noises while giving him head, making sure he could hear the smacking of her lips to play on his sense of hearing with erotic sounds. Amadeo called out Amy's name and said he was about to cum. Then he climaxed vociferously, squirting his juice into her hand like an erupting volcano. They showered, headed to the rooftop Jacuzzi, going in hard with round two. After a night of hot, steamy sex, they laid together kissing until they fell asleep.

In the morning, Amadeo asked her, "When can I see you again?" He laughed and added, "Can I have that coffee now to wash down that pie?" They both laughed and Amy brewed some fresh coffee. They chatted and agreed to see each other on Wednesday night. As soon as he left, Amy called Kayla to tell her all about her amazing date and sexy nightcap with Amadeo.

As the day went by, Amy was on Cloud 9 thinking about the fun she just had experienced with Amadeo. Then a text message came through and snapped her out of her reminiscing. It was from the other hot guy, Giovanni, the one she met at the mall who saved her from her epic fall. He wrote, "Hey there, beautiful! This is Giovanni, the almost superhero guy that saved you from that horrifying fall yesterday! Lol! How are you today? And when are you available to meet me for a night out?"

Amy wanted to see what he was about, so she told him she could meet Tuesday night—"just let me know where, and the time." He told her where and when, then mentioned for her to wear a dress as he was taking her somewhere fancy. Amy rolled her eyes and said to herself, what a cornball. He must not know about me, lol. She brushed it off as his good looks and his sense of humor charmed her. They chatted for a few minutes and decided on a 7 p.m. meeting at Red Lobster. While Giovanni said he would meet her there, he was only being playful—his real plan was to take her to The Penthouse at Mastro's in Beverly Hills. Amy and Giovanni got off the phone all smiles.

Amy had a good day at work on Tuesday then quickly jetted home to prepare for her night out with her hero. She showered, rubbed on her Dior body lotion, and slipped into a sexy coral bandage dress with side fringes that she recently ordered from VIP Divas Boutique. It fit her body like a glove, showing all of her curves. Then she slid into a sleek pair of nude Michael Kors peep-toe pumps. She knew she was a little over dressed for Red Lobster, but figured Giovanni had something up his sleeve because a man wearing Balmain shoes and a diamond Rolex is not impressing a woman like Amy on their first date with dinner at Red Lobster. She admired herself in the mirror one last time and headed out.

She arrived at the restaurant, parked then texted her hot date to let him know she had arrived. "Hey love, I'm here. I'm sitting in a white Range." She anxiously watched her phone, waiting for his response. Then she saw a white Phantom pull right in front of her. Who walked out? No one other than Giovanni. He had this huge grin on his face and tapped on her window and said, "Excuse me Miss, are you here alone?"

Amy laughed and replied, "Hmmm, just waiting on my lame date. He is ten minutes late but you are looking rather good." They both laughed. Giovanni told her to park and get her things as he had big plans for her that night. He stood patiently waiting for his blonde bombshell as she exited and secured her vehicle. Giovanni opened her door and handed her a single pink rose. Amy was star struck. Giovanni wasn't a famous Hollywood actor but he looked like he belonged on the big screen, looking dapper in a gray buttoned-down collared Burberry shirt with tailored slacks and Italian leather shoes. He told Amy how beautiful and stunning she looked. And she told him how handsome and nicely dressed he was. She also thanked him for her rose. Their ride to Mastro's was full of laughs.

They pulled up to the restaurant's entrance. The valet knew Giovanni and gave him a high five, exchanged words in Spanish and laughed. Amy wished she had Kayla with her to be her translator. Giovanni took Amy's hand as they entered the restaurant. Everyone there treated him like royalty. The hostess greeted him with a hug and quickly sat the pair, not in the regular dining area but in the private Penthouse section of the restaurant. Giovanni had gone all out and booked for private dining so he and Amy could truly have a special night, one on one. The waiter came right over and shook Giovanni's hand and told Amy she was a lucky woman. Amy just couldn't stop smiling.

Giovanni was attentive to Amy the entire night. He leaned in close, listening to every word Amy said. He pulled out the red carpet for her, having blanketed the entire room with an order of ten dozen roses for their dining experience. He had selected bottles of Veuve Clicquot and what appeared to be a sampling of the entire menu. They both enjoyed each other's company, equally mesmerized by their good looks. At the end of dinner, Giovanni told Amy that their night wasn't over—he had a friend performing a late show at the Improv on Melrose. Amy hesitated since she had to work in the morning. Giovanni gave her a long face and poked out his lower lip. "I live close by the comedy club. Come on, it will be fun," he said.

"I'm sorry, love, it's a Tuesday," Amy replied.

He then started singing, jokingly, "I thought we were about to have the club going up on a Tuesday." They both laughed, then he said, "OK, I understand. How about you come over for another drink and more conversation. I promise to have you home by midnight. My house is in the hills and has a beautiful view of the city."

Amy smiled and accepted his offer. They drove over to his house, parked in the driveway and Giovanni escorted her in. "Welcome to my bachelor's pad, with hardly any furniture in it!" he laughed, adding, "Maybe you can help me decorate in here one day."

Amy laughed too and told him, "Yes, I see that my decorative skills might be needed in here!"

They both laughed and Giovanni walked Amy into his lounge area.

Amy has dated all types of successful men, but she was really impressed with Giovanni. He was successful but didn't brag like the other guys. He didn't tell her upfront about his financial status, his car or living arrangements and she liked that. Giovanni was talking as he walked her around, but Amy was daydreaming about how she could see herself all up in this man's house, driving his car and taking her friends for a ride.

Giovanni said Amy three times until, finally, she heard him and responded. "Huh, I'm sorry. I have a lot on my mind. Like how am I going to get up in the morning?" He laughed and asked her what type of drink she would like. She stepped over to his bar and sat on a stool then said, "Surprise me. Something with a kick to it but a little sweet."

He replied, "I have the perfect drink for you gorgeous!" He mixed up a concoction, shook it up, then poured it over two glasses of ice. He handed Amy a glass and said, "Let's toast to meeting by chance, good times, and a new friendship!"

They toasted to that and sipped on their drinks, then Amy asked, "What is this cocktail called? It's really good!" He says, "It's what I call a Muscle Relaxer! It goes down smooth and gets you in the mood, nice and relaxed."

Amy laughed and said, "In the mood, huh? You might be right because I'm starting to feel it. You're not going to try and take advantage of me are you?"

They both laughed and Giovanni said to her, "Of course not. I won't do anything to you that you don't want me to do. So is there anything you want me to do to you right now?"

She blushed and looked at her almost empty glass and said, "I'd like for you to come over here and give me a kiss!"

He quickly walked around from behind the bar and lightly touched her by the sides of her face and kissed her softly. She began to take hold of his strong muscular arms as the kissing became more passionate and intense. He picked her up sideways holding her in his arms and looking into her eyes, and then laid her on the couch, spread her legs and moved her black thongs to the side, while he began playing with her kitty. Then he put his face in between her legs and kissed on her soft thighs, kissed her lower lips and slid his tongue inside. He took her panties down and opened her legs wide, then he sucked on her kitty and pinned her down so she couldn't move, then he lifted her up slightly from her bottom and started licking the crack of her ass, just like the lyrics to that song by Khia, "My Neck, My Back, My Pussy, and My Crack." He went back and forth to her kitty and licked her clit then sucked on it until she came. Amy moaned and squirmed backwards from the feeling.

She told him that she wanted to return the favor. But he told her it was too late—he already came from pleasuring her. Amy said she was glad he enjoyed it as much as she did. Giovanni then got up to get two washcloths, wet them, and after he cleaned himself, he used the other wet cloth to clean her. She got up and kissed and hugged him, thanking him for being so considerate and for a great night. She started to rub on his cut up chest, then moved down to his stiff hard penis and stroked it, feeling how thick and long it was. She got excited and went down to get a closer look at it. She told him how beautiful it was, then she softly kissed on it, admiring ever inch of his thickness. She then sucked on it, getting it super wet and slippery. He moaned, ran his hands through her hair and then pulled her up, asking her to turn around and get on her knees. She followed instructions while he moved behind the bar and got a condom.

He came back over. Amy was on the couch and on her knees, with her back arched. She was looking back at him as he put on the condom, then slid inside of her and began to slow grind. The feeling of being inside of her was amazing. He couldn't control himself and started going faster and harder, grabbing her hair in a circular motion, wrapping it into his hand, then pulled her head back and leaned in close to the side of her face and loudly asked her, "Do you like how I feel inside of you? Is it hitting your spot, baby?"

Yelling out, she replied, "Yes! Yes, don't stop! It feels so good, please don't stop!" He went in with deeper strokes then slowed down in a rhythmic motion, going in and out while they could both hear that wet juicy sound splashing with each stroke. He announced that he was about to cum, then climaxed and held her tightly while her body shook. They lay there amazed at how good the sex just felt. Amy kissed him then went to clean up. Giovanni invited her to stay the night if she would like, but Amy declined, reminding him she had to be to work early and needed to head home. They hugged for a while before heading back to her car.

Amy drove home thinking about how much fun she just had and definitely wanted to see Giovanni again.

The next day she got a text from Giovanni telling her how much he enjoyed being with her and wanted to see her again soon. She was at work blushing and reminiscing. She had almost forgotten about her other friend, Amadeo, who she had a date scheduled with that night. Amadeo right then sent her a text, saying that he was thinking about her, and couldn't wait to see her later. And he asked her to call him so that they could figure out where to meet. After Amy saw the message, she called him from her work phone. He answered and they chatted, inquiring how each other's day was going, and then Amadeo asked her if she'd be able to meet him for drinks for a happy hour at the popular Beverly Hills lounge, Sidebar. He told her that a few of his friends would be there if she wouldn't mind coming around to meet them. She accepted and agreed to meet him there at 6 p.m. straight from work. But being the type of woman Amy was, she of course went home first, freshened up and touched up her makeup. Then she was on her way to the lounge.

She arrived, wearing a two-piece charcoal gray pencil Ann Taylor skirt suit with a pair of black patent pumps. She looked sharp, on her A game, causing a buzz when she walked in the room as always. She saw Amadeo at the bar, walked up to him and gave him a hug and a kiss on his cheek. He was excited to see her and started introducing her to one of his friends named Jonathan, and his wife, Kelly. They were a very attractive couple. Kelly, who was Filipino, was strikingly beautiful, and had the most flawless golden skin and shiny jet-black hair. Her husband Jonathan looked like he could be one of Amadeo's relatives. Amy was happy to see her new friend had good taste in friends. The two couples took shots, got to talking politics and sports. Amadeo was interrupted with a phone call, he was very quick, then he told Amy that his best friend was on his way and he wanted him to meet her. She told him she couldn't wait to meet him, too, and they ordered more drinks. About an hour or so later, Kelly and Jonathan left. They said they needed to go pick up their kids from Kelly's mother's house. Amy really enjoyed the couple's company and gave them a hug goodnight.

A few minutes after Kelly and Jonathan exited, Amadeo's best friend showed up and walked over to the bar. To his surprise, he noticed Amy sitting beside Amadeo and recognized her. As he approached them, a feeling of confusion came over him. Amy turned and saw him right in front of her. She almost spat her drink out into his face. It was Giovanni. Amadeo asked if she was OK, and then introduced her to his best friend.

Giovanni laughed and said, "Crazy coincidence, we've already met." And Amy was red in the face and really didn't know what to say at that point. She was about to melt with embarrassment.

Amadeo chuckled and asked, "Oh, wow. Well, how do you know each other?"

Giovanni turned to Amy and asked, "Should I tell him, or do you want to do the honors?"

She was starting to sweat and replied, with her voice shaking, "Well, ugh, I met him, ugh, a few days after I met you, and we actually went out for drinks. Um...this is so awkward."

She put her head down in the palms of her hands and exhaled.

Amadeo was a little upset, but he said to her, "Wow. This is crazy. Giovanni and I always liked the same type of women, ever since our college days. Well, this *is* a bit awkward." Then he thought, and quickly added. "But I'm known for improvising and just thought of a solution. Giovanni and I are best friends and we don't mind sharing. We haven't shared in a long time, so if you're interested in trying something new, the three of us can have some fun together."

Amy was shocked. She was not expecting this type of reaction from them. Amy sat there confused, and to a degree, she was offended. Inside, she asked herself, what type of whore do they think I am? Just because I gave you some pie and let you taste the kitty doesn't make me loose, does it? On the other hand, she did secretly have a fantasy of sleeping with two guys at the same time.

Giovanni broke Amy's internal conflict and said, "I'm down for that. No problems on my end. That's why we're best friends, we have a great understanding."

Amy responded, "Are you guys for real? You want to have a threesome with me? I mean, what type of woman do you think I am?"

"A grown one," Giovanni said.

Amy shook her head and said, "So you're not mad that I'm seeing both of you? This is insane."

Amadeo assured her that it was cool and they wouldn't mind fulfilling a dream. He told her, "Amy, have you ever had a fantasy about being with two attractive guys, both pleasing you at the same time?"

"Yes, but I'd never ask anyone to do something like that," she replied. "I don't know how I feel about this."

Then Giovanni said, "You don't have to ask, we're offering to make that fantasy a reality, if you want it."

Amy was still in disbelief of what was going on. She didn't know what to think. But she began imagining the both of them kissing, rubbing, and sexing her at the same time. She started getting a tingling feeling between her legs! She began discussing details with them, asking a few questions as to how this would go down. They convinced her to take a chance and give it a try. She agreed to do the threesome only if they promised to never tell a soul. They did, of course, and left the bar and jumped into the Phantom. Giovanni asked Amy to get behind the wheel and drive to his house. Feeling nervous, and excited, she still couldn't believe that she was about to have a threesome with the two hot guys she just started seeing. They knew each other and happened to be best friends—wow, this shit is crazy! Giovanni, meanwhile, jolted Amy from her thoughts. He couldn't wait to get to the house. He pulled out his large hard penis and took one of Amy's hands off the steering wheel. He had her feel the stiffness of his manhood. He guided her hand up and down his large thick shaft. She did the job as he squirted the sticky cream all over her hand. Then in a stern voice, he told her to put and keep both of her hands on the steering wheel. He leaned over and grabbed her right breast out of her shirt, exposing her large melon. He caressed it gently. Amadeo, watching the action from the backseat, told Giovanni to make sure he played with her pussy to get it nice and ready.

Giovanni told his best friend in a joking tone, "Don't tell me what to do. This isn't freshman year, I got this." He moved his hands down in between her legs and stroked her kitty. Amadeo instructed Amy to drive faster. Turned on by the urgency in his voice, she floored it, all while trying to safely drive the Phantom with the foreplay session in full effect.

They arrived at the house hot and aroused—it was time to go from appetizer to entree. They went inside and Giovanni served up some drinks, including shots of Patron Silver. Shortly thereafter, they headed upstairs to the bedroom. The guys immediately started taking off their clothes as if it was routine for them. Amy was nervous and still trying to come to the reality of what was actually happening. Recognizing that she might need some reinforcement, the guys both approached her, trying to make sure she was at ease.

They started by helping Amy remove her clothes. Amadeo was kissing on her thighs as he pulled down her pretty pink lace panties, while Giovanni was kissing her on her neck from behind and started unstrapping her bra. She was overwhelmed with pleasure, as they kissed and sucked all over her body. They climbed on the bed and Amadeo laid Amy back while using his two fingers to part her wet box. He slid his fingers inside of her gently. He took his fingers out and licked them, saying how good her juices tasted. Then he started kissing and sucking on her kitty. The awkwardness faded as the ecstasy escalated.

Giovanni watched and started kissing her deeply, as well, and biting her lips, pulling her hair, grabbing himself and stroking his pleasure tool. Then he put his stick in her mouth and she started sucking on it. Her saliva glands were working in overdrive as her mouth was dripping wet, spilling down onto her massive mounds all while she was about to cum from Amadeo's kisses down low. The sensation of getting pleasured orally while having her mouth full took her over the edge. The feeling of both acts truly drove her insane as her body shivered. Amadeo switched with Giovanni, putting himself in Amy's wet mouth while Giovanni put on a condom and entered her. He started stroking that kitty with his big thick throbbing penis. He plunged deep into her tight, wet walls and gave her a few hard strokes, then took his large penis out to tease her. He rubbed her clit until she demanded that he put it back in. He quickly slid back inside of Amy and drove even deeper in and out of her. Amy tried to express her pleasure, but the thick nine-inch Italian power tool in her mouth muffled the sounds.

Amadeo took his shiny penis out of her mouth and put on his armor. Then told Amy to get on top of Giovanni and instructed her to grind on that dick. Amy complied and rode his penis like she was a jockey in the Kentucky Derby. Amadeo grabbed her hips from behind to slow down the pace and puts some lube on his penis, then slowly entered her tight ass, while Giovanni was still in her kitty. Amy was in pure bliss! All you could hear were the sounds of wetness and moans from all three parties. Amy had never felt this good, and moved in ways she had never moved. The guys were both filling her up with their thick joysticks. The sounds, sights, and pressure were so intense Amy couldn't control herself. She was so turned on she dug her head deep in Giovanni's chest and screamed she was about to cum. Then she had the biggest, most explosive orgasm she had ever had in her life! Double penetration from two gorgeous men. Her mind was blown. Her fantasy was fulfilled and then some. Both of the guys exited her pleasure holes, pleased by the satisfaction expressed and evidenced by the wet squirts Amy expelled during her organism. Giovanni asked her to open her mouth and they both took turns getting oral pleasure from Amy. She handled both of their tools like a pro. She must have learned a lot from watching porn from those X-rated websites. She pulled, slurped and sucked until they both climaxed.

Their unexpected meeting and discovery became an epic night, which led to an ultimate sexual encounter! Amy liked the feeling so much that after that night she saw them both together many more times. ...Oh, and separately too. She nicknamed them the Dynamic Duo! Double the pleasure, double the fun! Well, you know what they say: It ain't no fun if the homies can't get none. Yes, as she told her girls, it was two the hard way. ...

There Goes the Neighbors

Dasia and Antonio are one of my few couple clients that come in together to get styled. My longtime client, Aja, referred them to me. They come in every other Friday at 4:30 to get their hair done. Dasia prefers, a wash and roller wrap and Antonio gets his thug-life corn rolls. These two are creatures of habit and don't experiment or try anything new. During their last visit they shared a story with me that had me questioning how well do I know my neighbors? ...

Dasia and Antonio are in their early thirty's, married, and they just recently moved into a brand new home. They're new to the neighborhood and to the DMV area, so they don't know anyone really, and just speak in passing and keep to themselves. Dasia loves the new home, and likes the fact that everyone in the neighborhood seems so friendly.

Antonio is a steamfitter, Dasia is a dental assistant, and they both seem to be holding it down. Dasia and Antonio are both very attractive. Dasia is five feet three inches, with flawless brown skin, long flowing jet-black hair and has big hazel eyes. She has a bangin' petite shape, and the sister definitely looks like she puts in work at the gym. Her handsome husband Antonio, is five feet eleven inches, light skinned with hazel eyes, and has a great body, as well. So needless to say, they are both easily noticed by others.

One midsummer's day, Dasia and Antonio were outside doing some yard work, when two of their neighbors came over and approached them. "Hey, I'm Lance and this is my wife Tracy," the brother said. "We live a few houses down, two to be exact."

Dasia replied, "Hi, I'm Dasia and this is my husband, Antonio. Very nice to meet you." They all gave warm smiles in greeting each other.

Tracy then said, "We wanted to officially welcome you to the neighborhood, and invite you to our annual cookout. It's going to be this Saturday starting around three. We would love it if you guys could come." Dasia and Antonio both said thanks for the invite, and they agreed to come to the cookout.

Tracy in an excited voice said, "Yay! You won't regret it. We have this cookout every year and have a ton of fun. Get ready for shots and ribs that make you want to smack yo' momma." Both of the couples laughed, but then were interrupted as a blue minivan pulled into Tracy and Lance's driveway. Lance noticed the car and signaled to his wife that it was time to go. She looked disappointed, clearly seemed to force a smile and said, "Well, let me go. That's Lance's best friend Daryl and his wife. They have a new minivan and want us to go for a ride. Nice meeting you guys and I can't wait to have you over for some grown-up play time." The couple went off to meet their friends.

Dasia said to Antonio, "That was really nice of them to welcome us, and invite us to their cookout. I'll make some shrimp salad." Antonio thought that would be perfect. "Yeah that was cool of them, and please do make some of that shrimp salad! Emm, emm, emm, I love your shrimp salad, baby. You know that's why I married you girl." Dasia turned her face up and rolled her eyes. Antonio continued, "Oh, come on, just kidding, baby. You know I married you cause you fine and have all the qualities of a good wife."

Dasia smiled and said, "That's more like it. 'Cause I could let myself go and look like Tracy."

Antonio came back quickly and said, "And I could look like Lance."

While Tracy and Lance seemed to be really sweet and friendly, they were not the best lookers. Lance was about six foot one, balding, light skinned with terrible acne, and skinny chicken legs and a thick waist—the brother looked like he was about twelve months pregnant. Tracy was Asian—she looked like she could be from the Philippines or even Vietnam. And while her medium-length hair was styled nicely and reminded people of that Farrar Fawcett look, the sloppy attire she had on when they met did not flatter her thick body. She was five foot four, and had a huge stomach with tiny breasts and a giant ass for an Asian chick—yes, she had a true ghetto booty. You could see why Lance might be attracted to her—it was a case of it's your booty and not your beauty.

A few days went by and Saturday rolled around. Dasia hooked up her shrimp salad. She put on her favorite haltered-sundress that had a floral print, and her sexy black leather Steven Madden strapped sandals with the low classy heel. Her hair was in big soft flowing curls. She was glowing, looking absolutely gorgeous. Antonio also looked fresh with his swag on one hundred. Both were ready to meet and greet. They arrived at Tracy and Lance's house a little after 3:30, not wanting to be the first ones to arrive. They walked over with an old-school picnic basket containing the shrimp salad, and a bottle of white wine. They rang the doorbell and were greeted by Lance.

He said excitedly, "Come on in neighbors, glad you could make it! Oh, what did you bring?"

"Dasia's famous shrimp salad," Antonio said. "If you like seafood, you'll love it!"

Lance replied, "I do love seafood, can't wait to try it. We have a bushel of crabs, too. Come on out to the deck and I can introduce you to everyone."

They headed out back and Lance announced their arrival. Tracy was excited to see Dasia and Antonio, and came right over to greet them. She was showing her ass off by wearing a skintight purple mini-dress with a really low back. You could see all her rolls and dimples.

But beyond the host's fashion choice, it was a nice day, with a good crowd of guests. Everyone was talking, dancing, and the food and drinks were great. Tracy invited Dasia to help mix up some Patron Margaritas. They went to the bar and chatted and laughed about a few things such as their nosy neighbor, Ms. Bernice, that sits and watches everyone's comings and goings. Other ladies joined in their neighborhood gossip session as Tracy and Dasia continued mixing up drinks. The day flowed on with light-hearted chatter and food for days. Dasia and Antonio were loving their new friends and neighborhood.

As the day started to come to an end and the party died down, people were beginning to clean up and leave. Lance asked Antonio if they'd like to stay a little longer for another drink and so the guys could finish up the card game. Antonio agreed to stay. After the card game was finished, Lance asked Antonio if he wanted to see some pictures from the tropical vacation he and Tracy just returned from. Antonio said sure, and Lance broke out his laptop and pulled them up. The two of them started browsing through the photos while the ladies were inside sipping on their mixed drinks and chatting. Lance said, "Man, have you been to Jamaica? We really got loose there, mon." After his lightweight Jamaican accent, he gave Antonio an intense stare, and laughed.

Antonio responded, "No, but I always wanted to go. I hear it's beautiful and from these pictures, I really, really, want to go now."

Lance looked at the computer screen and said, "These pictures don't even give the Jamaican experience justice."

Then while looking at some of the photos, Antonio started to feel uncomfortable because the pictures started becoming X-rated. He clicked and saw a picture of Tracy on the beach with her small breasts exposed while she sat on an elderly white man's lap, who looked to be in his 70s. He said to Lance, "My bad. I think I clicked too far."

Lance said, "No, keep going, it's OK."

Antonio clicked again and again and came across pictures of topless women, couples half naked, and pictures of Tracy topless again with the same elderly man. But this time, Lance was also in the photo with both of his hands full. He had a drink in one hand and Tracy's plump-ass cheek in another.

Antonio was like, "Wow, man. I don't think I should even be looking at these kind of photos. That's your wife, man! I don't feel right looking at anymore. No offense, but I guess me and you think a little differently about those kind of things."

Lance apologized and said that they weren't afraid of showing off their bodies because they think nudity is beautiful. He also told Antonio that they go to nude resorts for vacations and flirt with other couples. Antonio told Lance that he didn't knock what they like to do, but he just wasn't as open to things like the way he was. And it was no big deal, to each his or her own. They ended the night and Antonio and Dasia headed home after thanking their hosts for inviting them, and telling them that they had a great time.

After making it home, Antonio told Dasia about the crazy photos. She was shocked, and said that she didn't think that they were those types of people. Dasia still thought that they were good people, but just very liberal. Antonio said, "He showed me a pic of Tracy topless with her boobs out; she was sitting on a geriatric patient, and she only had a damn thong on. Way too much! But I couldn't help but look. Her ass is phat as shit, though!"

They laughed hard and long, then Dasia said, "Shut up, boy, you're a damn fool! I can't believe he showed you a pic like that! You don't even like to show people my bikini pics from the beach!" They both continued to laugh while getting ready for bed.

A few weeks went by and Antonio had been trying his best to avoid Lance. He still felt uneasy about the pictures he saw at the cookout. Dasia was totally clueless of the severity of Antonio's feelings and accepted an invite from Tracy to come over for drinks and a card game. She excitedly greeted Antonio home and said she had plans for them to play cards with Lance and Tracy that night. Antonio snapped on Dasia, saying, "Why wouldn't you consult with me first before committing to go back over to our neighbor's house? I get a vibe from those two and I don't like it." Dasia and Antonio went back and forth over the invite for about twenty minutes. Exhausted from arguing, Antonio gave in. They got themselves together and headed over to their neighbor's house with the intentions of having a nice card game and a few drinks.

They were welcomed in by Lance. He was clearly overjoyed to have their company. He warmly welcomed them inside with a huge smile and invited Antonio and Dasia to have a seat. He broke out a bottle of Coconut Ciroc and everyone had a shot to get started on the card game. While playing a game of spades, they all laughed and joked with each other. They were having a great time. Lance turned on Pandora with his iPad and French Montana's song, "Ain't Worried About Nothin'" came on. Lance and Tracy started dancing. Then Lance mentioned wanting to really dance, and suggested they go party at this club that's always poppin'. He said it's a must-go-to spot, however, it's about an hour away from where they lived. Antonio was curious since he hadn't been out dancing in a while and he and Dasia love to party. He asked about the music and the cover charge.

Lance explained, "The club is called Vegas, and it's hot! The music is rockin' and the atmosphere is grown and sexy. Free for the ladies, and only ten for men before midnight. We should ride out there tonight, for real! What's up? Don't tell me y'all fakin'."

And with that said, everyone looked at each other, smiled, and in unison sang, "Ain't Worried About Nothin'." They took another shot and agreed to make a trip to Club Vegas. Lance offered to be the driver so that they could just all ride together to save time finding parking.

Once all piled in Lance's Honda Accord, Lance said excitedly, "The club is off the hook. There are two levels full of fun and anything goes in there."

Antonio squeezed Dasia's thigh and shot her a look of concern. So she asked, "What do you mean by 'anything goes?'" Tracy quickly interjected, "He means people get freaky on the dance floor, and drop it like it's hot! Everyone seems to have a good time dancing and partying with everyone."

Dasia then said, "Oh, OK, that's what's up! I can't wait to check it out and get my party on!"

Antonio agreed, adding, "You better drop it like it's hot all up on me girl!" He laughed and said, "I got a pole for you to work on!" He threw some singles in the air and everyone laughed as they continued riding to the club. Everyone was grooving to the music from WPGC 95.5, turnin' up to the Trey Songz track "Two Reasons" featuring T.I.

It wasn't long before they arrived at Club Vegas. The outside appearance made you feel like you were actually in Vegas. There were bright lights and gold nude statues at the entrance. The sign Club Vegas was huge and flashed in green and yellow lights. Lance decided to valet park since it was close to midnight. They got out and strutted to the red-carpet entrance. Antonio noticed a sign that said, "Members Only." He asked one of the bouncers, "Do you have to be a member in order to get in here?"

The bouncer replied, "You have to have a membership for VIP access, but not to get into the main area of the club. But I tell you what, I'll offer you a free membership because your girl is fine as shit. No disrespect intended."

Antonio answered, "Alright man, but be cool. *My wife is fine*, thanks. We just wanna go in and have a good time. I don't need a VIP membership."

Everyone laughed it off except for Antonio. Then Lance said, "No problem, man. Tracy and I have VIP memberships." They all showed their IDs and walked into the club.

As soon as they entered the doors, they could hear that the DJ was rockin'. And the two couples danced as they walked into the club. The sounds of Two Chains' "I Love Bad Bitches" featuring Drake, Kendrick Lamar and A$AP Rocky, especially got everyone hyped. The club was beautiful. Everything was plush and upscale, the lounge area had burgundy velvet chaise seating with gold accents, and there were huge chandeliers that guided patrons to the main area of the club. It all was modern and sexy, with flat-screen televisions encased in gold-detailed trim on every wall. There were sexy shadowbox dancers, and seductive vixens in cages moving their voluptuous bodies provocatively. The partying was hard from wall to wall.

Once inside the main room of the club, the group headed over to the first bar they saw and ordered drinks. The bartender greeted Lance and Tracy by name and said, "Hey guys. I haven't seen you two in a while. I see you brought friends this time." Tracy seductively put her index finger in front of her red lips and smiled. Lance yelled loudly, "All rounds of drinks on me tonight." Antonio and Dasia loved the treatment and with drinks in hand, they started vibing to the music and taking in the sights. The DJ put on "Blow the Whistle" by Too Short and the turn up was official. Several other couples greeted Lance and Tracy as if they were club celebrities.

Dasia was really enjoying herself and said to Tracy, "Thanks for the invite girl. Oh, this is my song," as Yo Gotti's "Act Right," played in the background. She put her drink in the air and swayed from side to side. She turned around and stopped dancing, as she for the first time took a good look at the dance floor. She focused her attention on two people dancing off to the side, and was in a state of shock from what the woman was wearing. She had on a black see-through, sheer dress with thongs and no damn bra! The guy had on a red-netted see-through top, tight leather pants, and a studded dog collar! She couldn't believe what she was seeing! She brought it to Antonio's attention, and as he caught the show, they both started taking a more thorough look around. It was a peak-a-boo dress code, which Lance and Tracy had failed to mention. Antonio and Dasia's jaws dropped when the DJ got on the mic and said, "For all you first timers and regulars, welcome to Club Vegas! What happens here stays here! Who's feelin' lucky tonight? Let's get it in!" Why did the DJ have to say that? At that moment all the TV screens turned from music videos to scenes of soft porn. Antonio and Dasia were starting to feel like Club Vegas was a Lance and Tracy set up. From the look of things it appeared to be one big swingers party! They spotted people dressed in sexy costumes, see-through fishnet and lace, leather and whips, pants with asscheeks cut out, and practically wearing undergarments! It hit them pretty hard as to what type of party they were in the middle of.

Antonio angrily said to Lance, "What is goin' on up in here? This is not what we signed up for. This is some shit! It's some straight freaks up in here!"

Lance laughed and in the most proper tone said, "The people who come here express themselves openly and have a good time. It shouldn't matter what they're wearing. The music is rockin', the drinks are great, so let's have fun and make the best of it and party!"

Tracy looked at Dasia with a bright smile and told her to follow her upstairs for a more chill setting. Dasia was still frozen in shock, full of confusion and didn't respond. Tracy grabbed Dasia by the arms and said, "Trust me. There are more private and chill areas upstairs." Then to her other half, she added, "Antonio, come on. Give it a shot, love."

Even though Dasia and Antonio were ready to leave, they decided to go upstairs to at least check it out before they gave up on the club. They figured that it couldn't possibly be any worse. They walked over to the elevator and there was a big bouncer, standing about six foot three, at the elevator doors. He looked like a former football player. He was big and stocky and looked hard. He greeted Tracy and Lance with a hug and asked to see their VIP cards. Tracy showed him her card and whispered in the bouncer's ear. His straight face lit up and he gladly opened the elevator door to the VIP level. As soon as the elevator doors opened there was calm. The music wasn't as loud as the first floor and it wasn't even packed. Everyone walked off the elevator and a thin blonde hostess approached the couples. She was wearing red nipple pasties with fringe that moved with each step she made and a short red and black apron that had embroidery writing, which read "Shhhh! Club Vegas." The beautiful blonde asked, "Are you familiar with our packages? Of course, you are. You two are practically here each week. Which package would you all be interested in tonight?" Tracy and Lance looked at each other and hugged, never answering the hostess. They whispered in each other's ears and then Lance spoke up and said, "We will be having the grand slam tonight. We want our guests to experience Club Vegas in its entirety." The hostess smirked and said, "Sir, the grand slam is our most expensive package. ..." Lance pulled out a stack of $100 bills and said, "I know, and that's what I told you we will be experiencing tonight."

The hostess rolled her eyes and placed black bands on everyone's wrists. Lance pulled out a black card and firmly held the blonde by the arm. His lips were tight and he said something to her in a low tone. No one could hear what he was saying but she looked nervous and apologized to all. Dasia and Antonio looked at each other and tried to play along.

The second floor was even more beautiful than the first floor. There were nothing but mirrors and nude marble statues. Lance led the group down a hallway where five different doors appeared to be lined up. Each door had a number labeled on them. Lance stepped in front of door Number One and turned around to thank his new friends for coming out with him and Tracy. He asked Antonio to enter door one with an open mind. Dasia squeezed her husband's hand tightly and he agreed he would. Antonio thought, what can be worse than porn on the screens downstairs. They all entered door one. Once inside there was nothing but another room with more mirrors. Lance said to the group, "Don't panic. I'm going to turn the lights off so the party can begin." Antonio became heated—when the lights were turned off you could see people were in another room with clear glass walls so that you could see what they were doing. It was like a human zoo. ...

Room one... There was a really attractive interracial couple making out in the room directly in front of them. The woman looked to be in her late-20s. She was Caucasian with beautiful long sandy-blonde hair. She was a big, beautiful woman with curves in all the right places. Her partner looked Latin—he was tall, dark and handsome. And with a buff body and muscles for days, he looked like a gym rat. The room looked like an outdoor-themed setting—with a park bench, fake trees, flowers and bushes. The sandy-blonde gave her Latin lover a sensual strip tease as Ne-Yo's "She Knows" played in the background. The girl had skills. She was extremely flexible and stood in front of her lover with one erect leg held straight in the air. She maintained her balance while standing in sexy six-inch red stilettos and twirled her shapely body. She then got on her knees and jerked her head from side to side, whipping her hair all about like a wild woman. Her lover sat there feigning in amazement of the show the beauty was putting on for him. The dancing queen looked up as if she could see the observing group through the glass. Then she unzipped her partner's pants and took his erect penis out of his jeans. Right when she started to engage in the sexual act the lights came on and their room went dark. Antonio shook his head as Dasia laughed. She was tickled by the action, but quickly hid it after seeing how pissed Antonio was. Tracy excitedly turned around and said, "You guys ready for room two?"

Room two… They entered and just as before, the room was nothing but mirrors. This time Tracy turned the lights out and there was a foursome going on. It was hot and heavy, literally. There were two couples engaging in kinky sex. The two men were handcuffed to a large bed while their partners were both riding them like two cowgirls. Antonio turned into the Incredible Hulk and told Lance and Tracy that they were getting the heck out of there, ASAP.

"No, don't be like that!" Lance said as he turned on the lights. "We can have fun together! We think you two are so hot, and we want to have a good time with you!"

Dasia was sickened by what she had just heard. Then Tracy chimed in and said, "Let me and Lance go down on you two. You don't have to do anything else if you don't want to. Just try to be open minded! Remember Antonio, you said you would have an open mind."

Antonio said, angrily, "If you two nasty-ass freaks think we would let you do anything to us, then you're fucking crazy." He looked at Lance and said, "I'll beat the shit out of your ass if you try some shit with my wife! You nasty, sick freaks. I see you tried to put us in a trick bag! I should mop your bitch-ass right now!"

"I can't believe you brought us all the way here and tried to recruit us. This was some fucked up shit!" Dasia yelled out.

Tracy burst into tears and said, "But...but...," Dasia cut her off and demanded for them to let her and Antonio out.

Lance pulled out his thick hard dick and said, "Dasia you know you want this."

Antonio rushed to Lance and punched him right in the mouth, knocking him out cold.

Dasia spit on Lance's limp body and screamed, "Don't you ever contact us again you sick, sneaky, down-low freaks!"

Antonio grabbed Dasia and said, "Let's get the fuck out of here before we catch a case."

They ran down the hallway towards the exit sign, escaping Club Vegas with all swiftness. They walked a little ways away from the club, and got on the Lyft app to get a ride. Even though the cost would be ridiculously high because they lived over an hour away, they didn't care at that point. They just wanted to get away from that crazy place and head home after that wild shit. The Lyft driver picked them up and said, "Let me guess—you guys just left Club Vegas?" Dasia and Antonio just looked at each other and laughed. ...

Still in a state of shock back at their home, Dasia said to Antonio, "Can you believe that foolishness? I'm still in shock from that shit!"

Antonio replied. "That was crazy insane. I still can't believe what just happened. What the hell was behind door five?"

Dasia laughed and said, "Probably some farm animals."

"But babe, I saw you get turned on when Lance pulled out his dick," Antonio said with a smirk.

Dasia laughed some more, and said, "Shiiit...But if they were more attractive, we might have considered it! Their funny-looking asses? Hell no!"

Dasia and Antonio continued their deep belly laughs, while laid back on the family-room couch. Then Antonio said: "Well damn— there goes the neighbors!"

Who the F*ck Did I Marry?

Mya was one of my first clients after I completed cosmetology school. She came from a very strict and religious family. I truly think her sheltered upbringing caused her to be so naïve to dudes running game. I saw her go through many hardships in her relationships with men but nothing like the struggle with her husband, Jessie. ...

Mya and Jessie were the picture perfect couple. They started dating their senior year at Morgan State. He was the star football jock and she the homecoming queen. After graduating college they got married and started their family right away. Jessie always treated Mya with the utmost respect and their sex life was bananas.

Mya would often brag to her friends about how good Jessie was in the bedroom. Especially, giving him praise on his "good head." She said his head was the best she had ever had, and every time he tasted her love she wanted to leave him a tip on the nightstand. After five years of marriage, two kids, a beautiful new home and successful careers, Jessie and Mya seemed to have it all together.

But the sad truth was that Mya was starting to feel distant from Jessie, and started seeing changes in his actions and his attitude towards her. When she walked in a room and he was on the phone or computer he would quickly get off. He also put a lock on his phone, which is something he and Mya said they would never do. Mya started to feel the words Tamia sang on the radio as she was riding home from a long day of work: "There's a stranger in my house." She was trying to get in touch with Jessie all day and was in deep thought because this was a pattern that was starting to repeat itself and become all too familiar.

Jessie started focusing less attention on Mya and more attention on his new office friends and after work "networking" activities. The weird thing is Jessie never introduced her to his new friends. In fact, when she confronted him about why she hadn't met them he almost transformed into a monster, like Dr. Jekyll and Mr. Hyde, put up a big protest and downright refused to answer. He would often say, "You don't have to know all of my friends, I don't know all of your friends." However, that was a lie. Jessie knew all of Mya's friends and she always included him in her activities. She was just sick of the secrets, excuses and lies. Mya made up her mind: Tonight was the last night for him to come home late with a day of him ignoring her calls. It was time to confront the man who made her his wife.

Mya prepared dinner, put the kids to bed and waited for Jessie to come home. He came in around 4:00 a.m., startled to see Mya still up. By this time, Mya was on level ten. Her pretty peach complexion was red from her being so upset. In a low voice, she said, "Jessie Anderson, do you know what time it is? This is the last time you are going to come in this house late and disrespect me and our children."

Jessie did not respond. He had a stupid look on his face and said, "Mya, it's too late for us to be talking about this shit. Why the fuck did you stay up? Last time I checked, I was a grown-ass man. Don't you like living in this big-ass house?"

Mya raised her voice and yelled, "Nigga, I work just as hard as your ass and pay almost half of the mortgage and other bills. I know your monkey ass ain't going there."

Jessie was shocked because Mya had never talked to him that way. Lost in thought, Jessie grabbed Mya's ass and said, "Damn, that's some sexy shit. I never seen you take charge like that. I like it!"

Mya pulled away and said, "Don't fucking touch me. You don't deserve to touch me tonight, after the way you been treating me."

Jessie moved in closer and said, "Girl, come here. Don't be like that. I got busy at work and my boss asked me to go with him to entertain some clients. We all got on the vice president's boat and ended up at Proud Mary for dinner. You know Bob loves the Bloody Mary's and crab cakes from there. We all had to force him to leave. After that we had to take the boat back to the dock in Georgetown. We were all drunk so I decided to sleep it off a little. I promise to do better, baby. I was trying to close this deal. You know my job requires a lot of schmoozing." He gave her that look that made Mya melt.

Mya stared at his beautiful green eyes and whispered you promise. He shook his head yes and told her that he loved her and she was his heart. He then got on his knees and pulled up her floral printed nightgown and started softly kissing on her inner thigh. As she fake resisted, he pulled her closer and grabbed at her panties, pulling them down her big round ass. He slipped his tongue in her freshly shaven peach. Mya moaned with pleasure as she gave in to what he did best. Jessie stayed on his knees pleasuring his wife, licking and sucking all of her sweet juices. He licked her sticky wet clit and twirled his tongue around in a motion that drove Mya crazy. She moaned as Jessie drove his head deep into her wetness. Mya screamed out and climaxed in Jessie's mouth. Jessie laughed inside because he knew exactly what to do with his head game to make Mya happy.

Jessie said, "Now it's time for me to have a little fun." He stood up, and took off his clothes, standing under a dim light, looking just as he did back in his football days. His tall six-foot-two frame, with the definition of a perfectly chiseled statue, stood over Mya. As they locked eyes, she could not resist the man that she always loved. Deep down inside she didn't want to give him her goodies, but her pussy was pulsating and craved his chubby eight-inch thick dick. Mya unzipped Jessie's pants, put her hands down his boxers and freed his big juicy cock. She dropped to her knees ready to pleasure her man. Her excitement was uncontrollable as she licked, jerked and sucked his manhood. However, there was a problem—Jessie was not getting hard. Mya just didn't understand. She was always able to get her husband hard. Jessie could sense her frustration and stopped her from stroking his dick. He said, "Baby, give me a minute to shower and get myself together. I promise to be out in a few minutes. Keep that pussy wet so I can dive in." He excused himself and went into the bathroom for a pep talk. Jessie took a Viagra, hopped in the shower and came back into their bedroom ready to put in work. Let's just say that make-up sex was in full effect. They spent the night making passionate love, hitting every position, even ones they never experienced or knew they could even do.

Even after a night of passion, Mya still had thoughts running through her head about what was happening to her marriage. She walked over to her co-worker Tonya's office for some advice. Tonya had been married for eighteen years and seemed to still have a solid relationship with her husband. Mya looked up to Tonya like a big sister. Mya confided in her friend of the noticeable changes she was seeing in Jessie. Tonya suggested she and Jessie get away. Tonya shared that whenever she and her husband had issues in their marriage they would try to get away for some alone time.

Mya was excited about the idea of getting away with her man, just the two of them, to try and spark up their love life. She left Tonya's office and spent most of the day searching for deals online and finally found something worth booking with Southwest Vacations. She called her mother and made arrangements for the kids. Everything seemed to be right on track, until trying to get in touch with Jessie, which was once again a mission impossible. He was back to his old routine. It seemed like their lovemaking last night did not matter. His promise was quickly forgotten. Poor Mya thought she made a breakthrough with her tough-girl confrontation. She thought Jessie was going to start spending more time with her right where he needed to be. But 10:00 p.m. rolled by and there was no Jessie. He didn't answer her calls nor did he respond to any of her text messages asking why he was unavailable. He just sent her a text to say, "Working late. See you when I get home."

This time Mya said she was going to play it cool, just sit back and observe his behavior. She was determined to get down to the bottom of this. As soon as Jessie arrived home shortly after midnight, Mya laid in the bed pretending as if she was asleep and made a mental note of the time. The next morning, she put on her good wife face and said, "Good morning, baby. You must have had a hard long day at work yesterday. I missed you again last night. Well, I'm excited to tell you that I booked a relaxing get away because I feel that this is something we both need. I already made arrangements for the kids to stay with mom and here is the itinerary for our trip."

Jessie was cold and just stared at the itinerary. He finally responded, "I can't go. I got a lot going on with the job with this special project. You know I'm trying to close this deal. I'm on a tight deadline, and these dates won't work. Why didn't you include me in the planning?"

Jessie's tone was serious, which hurt Mya's feelings. "This was supposed to be a surprise, baby, that's why I didn't include you in the planning. I thought you would appreciate this and would be super excited. Plus, when I tried to reach you there wasn't an answer." Mya tried not to cry but she couldn't fight back her tears.

Jessie put on a fake smile and said, "OK, baby, I'm sure I can work something out. I really do want to go on this trip. Don't worry your pretty little head about it. Let me see if Bob can take over my caseload while we're away. I do appreciate everything you do for me and our family." He kissed her on the cheek and prepared to head out for work.

"Flight 257 Miami, boarding Gate 7." Those were the sweetest words Mya could have heard. She had big plans to enjoy quality time with Jessie: no deadlines, no kids, no mystery friends. It was all about her and Jessie for five days. Mya was ready to get that old thing back and packed toys and other fun items for her and her hubby to partake in.

When they arrived on Ocean Drive, the weather was about 85 degrees. It was much better than the bitter cold they left behind in DC. Jessie grabbed Mya's plump ass as they were walking down Ocean Drive taking in the sights and could feel that Mya didn't have any panties on. He said, "Girl, you know what you do to me when you go commando. Let's get a drink over at Wet Willies, so I can get right from this flight and lay that ass down." They walked over to Wet Willies and it was a real different crowd in the building. There were some loud ghetto hood fats—yes, hood fats because these chicks had rolls for days and weren't afraid to let it all hang out (don't get it twisted, ain't nothing wrong with big girls; but just saying, some things are not for everybody). These chicks had on bikini tops with denim boy shorts. There was also a group of transgender men that were not hard to notice. One stood about five feet and wore some blonde tracks and had curves like Nicki Minaj. The other two were about five foot nine and dressed in women's designer clothing from head to toe. It looked like the Off Saks exploded and all the labels landed on them.

Mya noticed that Jessie kept glancing over at the table with the transgender men. She joked, "Wow, babe. Maybe I'll get some Chanel shoes like 'Nicki' over there."

Jessie laughed and said, "Yeah, I was just laughing at those clowns, trying to see which part of their designer pieces I can get for you, boo." They both laughed and continued to down their drinks. Mya was feeling a buzz and got up to go to the bathroom. She was gone about ten minutes because she was really feeling those drinks and had to take a moment to get herself together. To her surprise, when she returned Jessie was nowhere to be found. She scanned the room and then saw him over at the table with "the clowns." Mya was puzzled and slowly walked over. When Jessie saw her he quickly got up and greeted her. He introduced his new friends to Mya. "Nicki" rolled her eyes and said, "Hi beautiful. You got a lot to handle with this big guy."

Mya gave the blonde woman-man a smirk, and said, "I sure do!" Mya saw their waiter bringing their food out and saw this as a perfect opportunity to get out of this awkward moment. She turned to Jessie and said, "Oh babe, I see our food is coming out. Nice to meet you all." Once back at their table a curious Mya said, "OK, what were you doing over there with those 'clowns?'"

"Well, I went over to really ask about the Chanel shoes for you, babe," Jessie said. "I know how you love your Chanel. Mya grinned and said, "Yeah, those shoes are hot. You better get those for me, daddy." They both laughed and signaled the waiter back to their table for another round of drinks. As they sat at their table, Mya felt someone staring at her. When she looked back it was the short guy with the blonde wig. She chalked it up to a chance glance and laughed it off. "Jessie, see you should have never asked about those shoes. Now you got a secret admirer. Nicki 'Mirage' is over there staring us down, geesh."

Jessie chuckled at her play on the Minaj name, and jokingly added, "Really? Oh, you jealous of Nicki aren't you? You got a little competition and don't like it, huh."

Mya looked back at the diva and replied, "Like you said, those shoes are hot." They burst into laughter, paid their bill and decided to hit the beach.

Jessie and Mya lay on the beach with their perfect bodies and smooth skin. Mya looked hot in her skimpy red Beach Bunny bikini. Jessie looked sexy with his dark chocolate body glistening in the Miami sun. He was looking oh so fresh with his Burberry swim trunks and shades to match. After his dip in the ocean, he walked out showcasing the outline of his large pole. Mya watched her man come out the water dripping swagoo. They laid out and swam for hours, having a blast spending quality time together. As the day turned to early evening they decided to wrap things up and head back to the room. As they gathered their items they noticed the blonde wig wearing transgender guy with a very masculine tall white man. The pair walked hand in hand along the beach. Mya was surprised because the handsome companion looked straight as a board; nothing about that man looked like he indulged in that lifestyle. She turned to Jessie and said, "Wow, I guess sometimes you just don't know."

Jessie gave her a stupid face and said, "What do you mean by that?"

"Never mind," she said. "Let's keep this trip all about us."

Jessie and Mya walked down the beach towards their hotel and saw some movement in the distance. As they walked closer to the figures, they realized it was the blonde guy and his buff date fucking on the beach in a dark corner by the public showers. The blonde was bent over in the zone and was getting slammed hard by the tall handsome guy. The grunting by the two men stopped Mya in her tracks. She had a shocked look on her face; she had never seen anything like that before. She took her phone out about to record the two men in their sexual act and announced to Jessie, "This one is for Worldstar." To her surprise Jessie had a look of pleasure on his face. He was in pure amazement of the act being performed. Mya was totally caught off guard. The man she knew would not have stood there to watch these two engage in this sort of sexual act. In fact, from the looks of things his manhood was rising. Jessie indeed seemed excited. Mya was disgusted while she watched Jessie stroke his penis through his shorts as if he was watching his favorite porno. She waved her hand in his face and he snapped out of his gaze. Jesse then said, "Come on babe. Worldstar ain't posting that video. Let's get out of here." Mya was confused by Jesse's behavior but kept her feelings to herself.

Mya and Jessie decided to go to Prime 112 for dinner after getting showered and dressed. She felt as if she was connecting with her husband over their meal, as they talked about their differences and what they wanted in their marriage. After all the serious talk and a few glasses of Birthday Cake wine, Mya was feeling naughty. She took her heels off and rubbed her beautifully manicured feet on Jessie's crotch. She rubbed and rubbed until she felt something stiff in his pants. She looked deeply in her husband's eyes and said, "Meet me in the bathroom and bend me over like the blonde on the beach, baby."

Jessie didn't like that. His face tightened and he knocked her feet off his lap. "What's wrong with you? How can you compare us to those two on the beach? You are my wife and those were two men getting it in. I knew you were going to bring that incident up. You are something else. I'm ready to leave."

Mya thought her joke was sexy and innocent. She felt like a complete failure as all sorts of emotions raced through her. Maybe we are done, she thought. I don't know how much more of this nasty attitude I can take.

On the ride back to their hotel the two were silent. They both stared out the window, ignoring one another. Once back in their room, Mya thought she would try to reach Jesse one last time. She remembered some of the tips her friend Tonya shared and thought to try one on Jessie that night. Maybe if I bring one of my toys out I can get him to open up, she thought. Mya eased the toy from her bag when Jessie wasn't paying attention and she slipped into the bathroom. She redid her makeup and stripped down to her birthday suit. Her sexy body emerged from the bathroom, taking Jessie by surprise. He truly wasn't expecting Mya to come out ready for sex. He noticed she had one hand behind her back and got a little nervous. His voice was shaky as he asked, "Babe, what's behind your back? I'm sorry about tonight. I didn't mean to go off on you like that."

"Shhhh!" Mya said. "Just relax. It's just a little prop for tonight." She put the toy down on the dresser and got down on all fours crawling to her mans lap.

She struggled to get Jessie's pants down so she could pleasure him with her mouth. Mya slid his big dick far back until the head nudged the back of her throat. She massaged and stroked his thick meat with her mouth. Again, Jessie struggled to get hard. Mya remembered a trick her friends told her, about licking underneath the balls to the anal area. She spread Jessie's legs and told him to lay back. She pushed his legs back and rubbed his balls with her hand as she worked that area with her tongue as her friends described. She even licked his ass a few times. Just like that his dick was hard. It was hard as a rock. Mya was pleased by the outcome. Jessie stood up and fucked Mya's face with his large dick. "Suck it, baby suck it! Oh fuck, I'm about to cum!!" Jessie moaned. Just like that he came in Mya's mouth. She enjoyed every drop.

She felt like a character from one of her favorite Zane books, getting down and naughty with her hubby. Mya looked up and said, "Are you ready for more, baby? I got so much more to give."

Jessie shook his head yes, and said, "Hey, I see you put a toy down over there. What's that?"

Mya replied it's called a bullet. Jessie got excited and said, "One of my co-workers at work said he and his wife use the bullet. Come bring it over."

Mya got up happy to hear her husband sound like he was actually interested in trying something new. She handed the bullet to Jessie. He turned the vibrator on and rubbed it around each of Mya's erect pink nipples. He then slipped one of her perky breasts in his mouth, then the other, licking and kissing each gently. He took the bullet and slid it down to her wet pussy. He rubbed the vibrator in an up-and-down motion on her clit. Mya came hard from the clitoral stimulation. Jessie whispered in her ear, "Now do me?"

A confused Mya said, "What baby? What do you want me to do?"

Jessie said, "I love how you licked and sucked my balls and ass. Can you do that again, but can you also rub the bullet down there, you know by my balls?" Mya, wanting to please her man, agreed. She sucked Jessie's dick real sloppy and rubbed the small vibrator against his balls. He grabbed her hand and moved the vibrator down lower, right around his asshole. He grinded and pumped his hips up and down as she sucked his dick. He pumped faster and faster, forcing his large dick deeper and deeper into Mya's mouth. Without notice, Jessie nutted in her mouth. Mya kept going. She continued to rub his balls and ass with the vibrator until he begged her to stop. He couldn't handle much more, as his body shook from the vibration that ran through his body. He cried out, "Oh shit, babe," and another huge gush a milky cream shot out. He came so hard he fell asleep shortly after their hot session—like a baby just having been fed a warm bottle.

The next couple of days in Miami were pure bliss. The two lovers seemed happy as ever. They partied and fucked like two 20 year olds. As their trip came to a close, it was bitter sweet as Mya knew in her heart there was a possibility this feeling of closeness would end. She was afraid of how Jessie would act once they returned to the DMV. Still, she was missing their kids and knew it was time to get back. All she could do was pray and hope for the best.

The first couple of weeks back from vacation Jessie was on his best behavior. He followed through on his promise and answered Mya's calls. He worked late but gave her advanced notice if he had to. He was home every night by eight. He even treated her to a spa day at her favorite nail shop Sassy Nails. Things were looking up, until May 1st, Jessie's birthday. He threw a huge birthday bash at Bar 7. He rented a car service for them so they didn't have to worry about drinking and driving. The kids were staying with her mom, so they could have the evening to themselves. He went all out and bought Mya this *bad* purple lace Versace dress with gray and purple Giuseppe Zanotti sandals. He had on this tailored gray suit with purple bow tie. The pair looked like they belonged on the red carpet at the BET Awards. When the car pulled up to the club, Mya took a sip of champagne and reapplied her lipstick to make sure she was looking her best. As she reached for her brush, she noticed Jessie was texting while looking out the window as if searching for someone. Mya just sat back in silence observing the situation. She saw this huge grin appear on her husband's face as if he was a kid at Christmas discovering the present he wished for. She looked out the window to see who had him smiling. To her surprise it looked like the transgender guy from Miami; this guy was rocking the same type of blonde wig. Mya gasped, Jessie then turned to Mya and said, "You OK, baby? Are you ready to make some people mad tonight?"

Mya quickly said, "Yes" and the driver got out to open her door. As soon as she stepped out she saw "Nicki Mirage" staring at her with a sinister look. Mya just shook it off and tightly grabbed her husband's hand. They walked up in the club right when the DJ dropped "Throw Some Mo" by Rae Sremmurd. The club went crazy. It was full of beautiful people, Mya felt like she was in a music video. She and Jessie walked to the back of the club to their table, which was full of family and friends. DJ Quick Silva had the club rocking, bottles were poppin', everyone was laughing and having a great time. That is, until Nicki Mirage and one of her plastic friends came over. Nicki screamed, "Jessie! Happy Birthday, Jessie baby!!"

Mya yelled over the music, "How can I help you, bitch? What are you doing here?" Jessie's brother tapped him as he could see Mya's head and hands moving all around, while the blonde stood there laughing steady, asking for Jessie.

"Get Jessie, bitch. I'm here for his muthafuckin' birthday!!"

Jessie walked over and said, "Jen chill!" Mya this is Jen from Miami. Remember her from Wet Willies?"

"Yes," Mya said, "but what the hell is he/she doing in DC at your birthday party?" At this time, Mya's crew of girlfriends all gathered around with all eyes on Jessie.

Jessie replied, "Well, Jen and I exchanged business cards in Miami. She called me last week and said she was coming up here for business. I mentioned my party and she said she would swing past for a drink. Is there a problem?"

Mya shook her head and said, "No, I guess not. I guess I should just shut up and be happy." She threw her glass of champagne in Jessie's face and stormed out the club. She caught a cab home and was in total disbelief that Jessie would embarrass her like that.

Mya just knew Jessie would walk through the door shortly after her, but no, that did not happen. Hours went past and no sign of or word from Jessie. Mya cried and cried. She was at a total loss as to what happened to the man she met many years ago at Morgan State. Her phone was blowing up with texts and phone calls from her girlfriends. She ignored each call. She would look at her phone hoping with each ring and notification it would be Jessie, but there was no sign of her man.

Mya grabbed a bottle of wine, popped a valium, ran her a warm bath and soaked in the tub while waiting for Jessie to come home. 6:45 a.m. rolled around and she heard the home security alarm chirp, as Jessie came through the door.

"Where the hell have you been?" Mya demanded. Jessie smelled like liquor and cheap perfume. His reflexes were still fast, though, as he ducked the empty bottle of wine Mya threw at his head and barely missed. Her eyes were red and puffy from crying and drinking all night. She yelled, "What is your fucking problem? Where is my husband? I want that nigga back 'cause I can't live like this." Luckily, the kids weren't there to hear them fighting.

Jessie said, "FUCK YOU BITCH. Thank you for ruining my birthday party." He turned around and walked out their bedroom door. She was heated and sat there in shock. Mya just knew he was coming back. A few moments later she heard the alarm door chirp again, she got up quickly, looked outside, and Jessie was driving off in his Jeep. Mya couldn't believe it. She immediately dropped to her knees and prayed. She cried and cried. Mya was lost as to what was going on in her home. She called Jessie, he answered and went off, "Bitch, don't fucking call me to say shit. You are wrong for putting on a show like that at my party. How dare you go off on my guest? I'll talk to you later." And like that he hung up. The reality that she and her husband were having major troubles hit her hard. Mya was a total wreck. She called Jessie back to back to back with no answer. She opened another bottle of wine, hit it hard and soon drifted off to sleep.

Early that afternoon, the phone buzzed and awakened Mya. Hours had passed since she and Jessie fought; so she was hoping it was him calling to talk, but it was her best friend Carmen on the line. Mya answered in a scratchy voice, "Hey sis, what's up?"

Carmen said, "You tell me. You left the club last night after getting into it with the girl in the blonde wig. You ignored my calls. What's going on girl?" Then she went on, "Your man was tripping last night. He ordered more bottles and had a group of suspect-looking people around him. He looked to be real cozy with that blonde chick. You know I had my cousin Vanessa with me last night—you know, the one who should have been an FBI agent—she swears she heard Jessie, his boss and that blonde girl talking shit. I mean nasty shit. Are you guys good? 'Cause I didn't like how he stayed and partied it up after you left the party upset."

Mya told Carmen about what happened when Jessie got home and everything else regarding his strange behavior. She complained how Jessie had been staying out late and coming in half drunk, trying to have aggressive sex with her, and trying to force her to have anal sex. She was getting tired of that shit, she said, "Why does he only get hard when he tries to force himself in my ass or when I play with his ass? He's been wanting to use the bullet more and more. I think he thinks this is Cell Block 8. I'm tired of this shit! It's OK getting some back action now and then, but this is fucking ridiculous."

Carmen listened and told her friend the hard truth—perhaps their marriage was over. They got married really young, right out of college. Perhaps they hadn't had enough time to enjoy and experience life and this was Jessie's way of getting a second chance to live his youth. Carmen could hear the hurt in Mya's voice as she responded defensively.

"How dare you judge me and my marriage?" Mya said. Carmen cut her off and told her to be strong and that she may want to consider separation. Carmen reminded her friend of her worth and that she deserved better than to be disrespected. Mya was mad at Carmen but knew she was right. She quickly got off the phone with her best friend and paced the floor of her 3,800-square-foot home.

Outside the house, she heard a car door slam. It was Jessie. Mya ran to the door and gave him a big hug. He too held her tightly and they both cried together. She then told Jessie she wanted a separation. Jessie cried and begged her to reconsider. He picked Mya up, threw her over his shoulder and took her upstairs to their bedroom. He laid her beautiful body on their king-size bed. Mya said, "No, this stops now. I don't want to have sex with you. I really want us to separate." Jessie ignored her and took off his clothes. He got on top of Mya and pressed his hot body against hers and nibbled on her breast. Mya screamed stop, and hit Jessie. He wouldn't stop. He stayed on top of Mya, desperately trying to kiss her. She moved her head away from him, and from side to side as he licked her face and tried to force his tongue in her mouth. This went on for about five minutes. She resisted and fought and fought. Tears ran down her face as Jessie aggressively tried to get her to fall into his usual trance. Jessie stopped and finally realized she really didn't want him. He apologized as Mya wept. She couldn't believe this was happening. Jessie slowly edged out the bed and slipped in the shower and said he had to go to work. Mya didn't respond, she just curled up in the fetal position and cried. Jessie couldn't stand to see Mya so hurt and decided it would be best to give her some space. Jessie said he was going away for a few days so they could figure things out and would be back once things had calmed down.

Two days went past with Jessie and Mya taking the time, separately, to think. She sat in her silent home wondering about the decline in her marriage. She tried her hardest to put the puzzle pieces together. She didn't understand why Jessie was always missing in action and couldn't stay hard for her. It was as if he wasn't attracted to her anymore. She thought maybe he was seeing someone else, and was just staying with her because of the kids and a basic comfort level. Mya being the researcher she is decided to look for a marriage counselor and review articles on saving a marriage. As she sat down with pen and paper, she attempted to log on to her home computer, but to her surprise the password had been changed. This took Mya over the edge. She called Jessie several times, but as usual there was no answer. Mya was extremely pissed and decided to call his job, something Jessie specifically instructed her to never do. She said to herself he is just going to have to forgive me.

A perky receptionist answered, "It's a great day at Goldberg and Associates. How may I help you?"

Mya replied, "I need to be transferred to Jessie Anderson, please. This is his wife and I have an emergency." There was an awkward silence on the line. An impatient Mya said, "Hello, are you there? I need Jessie Anderson, please."

The receptionist finally responded, "Yes, I'm still here. I'm sorry but Mr. Anderson is no longer an employee with Goldberg and Associates. I was looking to see if we had another contact number for you since you said it was an emergency."

Mya replied, "Excuse me, what do you mean he doesn't work there anymore?" The receptionist, fumbling over her words said, "Let me transfer you to the Human Resources Department."

Mya broke out into a sweat and a feeling of nausea came over her. The human resources assistant answered the line. It was a familiar voice. It was one of the HR assistants, Shelba. She had been working at the firm for years and helped Jessie add Mya and the kids to his health benefits plan. Mya also knew Shelba well as they both went to the same hair salon. So Mya was hoping Shelba could shed light on this situation. Mya said in a calm voice, and with familiarity, "Hey Shelba, how are you? This is Mya Anderson, Jessie's wife. I was calling to see if you could tell me what happened with Jessie losing his job? Jessie won't tell me and I need answers." Mya didn't tell Shelba that she didn't know until a few minutes prior about her husband's unemployment status.

Shelba whispered, "Girl, meet me at Park for Happy Hour at six tonight. I can't talk right now. And, anyway, I can show you better than I can tell you."

Mya quickly agreed to meet Shelba and hung up. She kept replaying the words "I can show you better than I can tell you" through her head. What exactly did Shelba mean? Six p.m. could not roll around fast enough. Mya wanted to see what Shelba had to show her. Mya had a glass of wine to help relax before getting dressed. Then she was off to the Park. When she arrived at the club in her shiny black Lexus GS, she had her car valet parked. The line for Park was wrapped around the building. But as soon as she hopped out her car, Mya being as fine as she was, quickly got waved down by the doorman to skip the line and come straight inside. She chuckled to herself, "Yeah, momma still got it." She was relieved she didn't have to stand in line. Mya walked in and all eyes were on her. She was feeling herself until anxiousness started coming over her at the sight of Shelba approaching. Shelba walked over and greeted Mya with a hug. "Hey girl, I got us reservations. I knew tonight would be super packed—Trey Songz is performing. I was just seated." Shelba led Mya to their table and got straight down to business. She said in her country accent, "Mya, girl, you know I can get fired for this, right? I'm just sharing this information with you because I considered you and Jessie to be the „it couple.' For years, I looked up to the love and marriage y'all shared. I always told people about you two. What he did is unforgivable. I don't even really want to show this to you but you need to know. These niggas ain't loyal!"

Mya leaned in close, hanging on to every word coming out of Shelba's thick candy red lips. Mya said, "Yes, I know you could get in trouble, so I appreciate you agreeing to share this information with me. I promise to never tell anyone that you told me what happened. I promise. But I really need answers. ..."

Shelba took out a large envelope from her tote bag and put a stack of papers in front of Mya and said, "Read!" Mya looked over the first paper and it was an email from Jessie's yahoo account to Mrazzsophat@gmail.com. In the email were details about Jessie and this person meeting for drinks in Miami. Mya looked at the date stamp of the email and it was during the time she and Jessie had been in Miami for their "Rekindle Weekend." Her jaw dropped when she read a telling line in the email from Jessie: "Yea, it really turned me on seeing you get fucked from the back. Can I get some of your truffle butter?"

Mya asked in an unbelieving tone: "What are you showing me?" Shelba replied with disgust, "Keep looking through the papers. Jessie was fired for inappropriate use of business funds and equipment. Yes, he used his personal email during office hours, but he spent hours and hours talking to this Miami person via email and on the phone. Jesse was one of our brightest black males in the company and he ruined everything. We also found that he used the company credit card to fund this person's travel. Look at this credit card statement. Isn't this the weekend of Jessie's birthday?"

Tears started falling down Mya's face as she reviewed the statement. Shelba continued, "Oh, don't cry just yet. We also have a transcript from a dating website he accessed during work hours. Read this, it's a damn shame." The document was a print out of Jessie's profile on a dating site. His profile picture was of his large erect penis. The profile read: *"Married, miserable black male, with BBC, looking for all my holes to be filled. I have a nice soft ass with curly black hair. I like giving and receiving."*

Mya spit out her drink. Now she knew exactly what her husband had been up to. He had been living a lie all these years. Mya turned to Shelba with a distressed look on her face and said, "Who the FUCK did I marry?"

Mr. Officer

Alisa is my girl. She has been a faithful client in my chair for years. She initially came to me as a shampoo assistant seeking work after moving to DC from the Bronx. Now she has another great job and comes to see me each week as a client. I look forward to her visits as she always brings me homemade Yucca Bread and tostones rellenos de picadillo...I hope I said that right... Lol! She moved to the DMV with her longtime boyfriend, Derrick. I never liked that guy, so when she told me about a wild experience she had that led to a steamy love affair, I must admit I was more than thrilled for her. ...

Alisa is a free spirited, opinionated, fun-loving girl that likes to enjoy life and the finer things in it. She is twenty-eight, one hundred percent Puerto Rican and proud. She stands five feet five, has big brown eyes, a golden-bronze complexion, and brown wavy hair. Her slim build and big boobs are the envy of many. She has one of those video vixen shapes with a super tiny waist and colossal ass. The girl is muy caliente! She is a kindergarten teacher who loves her job. She is dating her live-in boyfriend, Derrick, who is thirty, light brown skinned, thick with a nice build, and gorgeous green eyes. They've been dating for about eight years and have an interesting relationship full of ups and downs. But through it all, Alisa still wants more. She feels like after eight years it's time for Derrick to put a ring on it. But she's also dealing with trust issues with Derrick because of his past infidelities. Early on in their relationship, Derrick committed the ultimate betrayal with another woman. While he and Alisa were taking a break he was busy making a baby. He hid the baby from her and she only found out when they were out to dinner one night. As the waiter brought the food over to the table, a teary-eyed pregnant girl approached the table and exposed Derrick's secret. This along with countless other women over the years had caused Alisa much heartache. Lately Derrick had been staying out late and being more secretive of his whereabouts; when confronted he denied any wrongdoing. His actions were bringing suspicion and familiar memories back to Alisa.

Last night Derrick stayed out until three in the morning and his phone was once again dead. Tired of stressing over her relationship, Alisa said she was ready for a change. Instead of again staying home with Derrick to watch movies, she decided to get with a few girlfriends to hang out for a much-needed girls night. They went to their favorite spot in the city, StoneFish Grill, which is also a popular after work bar and lounge throughout the DMV. As they walked in they were singing along to the lyrics to Iggy Azalea's "I'm So Fancy"—the song was fitting as Alisa and her girls looked like they just finished a photo shoot. The girls were all so beautiful they broke necks as they pranced in the spot. Alisa and her girls wasted no time turning up. They ordered bottles, shots, hookah, and appetizers. The lounge had eye-candy galore! Alisa flirted with guys throughout the night, but this one she saw really caught her attention. Their eyes met and he started coming towards her. As he got closer, she realized that he was freakin' gorgeous! About six foot two, brown skinned, sexy thick soft lips, big strong arms, body bangin'! He came over and introduced himself in a deep voice, "Hello, gorgeous. My name's Sean, what's yours?"

Of course, she was in awe, admiring his handsome face and oh, so sexy body. She answered with a nervous laugh, "Oh, my name, is Alisa." They started a conversation that led to more drinking, to dancing, and more drinking and dancing. They had great chemistry. They exchanged personal information and ended the night with a close, tight, sensual hug. Sean also took advantage and kissed Alisa on her forehead, cheek and neck. Alisa's friends teased her the whole way home about this Sean guy. They jokingly sang, "Alisa and Sean, sitting in the tree, K-I-SS-I-N-G." They all laughed and headed home. Later that night, Alisa was at home, laying in bed alone, thinking about Sean's soft sexy lips, wondering what they'd feel like on her lips (all of them), K-I-SS-I-N-G.

The next day while Alisa was at the YMCA getting a good workout in, she received a text and realized it was from the hottie she just met. He asked how her day was and said he couldn't stop thinking about her. He asked if they could meet for dinner and drinks. Alisa, without hesitation, texted back, "Sure, I would love that..."

Sean replied, "Wassup with tonight?" They agreed and set a time to meet at Maggiano's Little Italy in Chevy Chase.

Alisa hurried home wondering what to tell Derrick. She just knew he would be upset about her going out two nights in a row. As she pulled her black Jeep Cherokee in front of her brick townhouse, she noticed she was home alone, once again. She called Derrick to tell him she was going out. Derrick screamed through the phone, "Hey babe." Loud music could be heard in the background.

Alisa said, "Hey you. I was calling to tell you I'm going out tonight for dinner with Jen."

"Huh! What..." Derrick replied. Alisa repeated herself louder and Derrick responded, "Oh, OK, babe. Have fun. I'm gonna text you. It's too loud."

A few moments later Derrick's text comes through, "Hey, sexy have fun with your friends. I'm sorry I couldn't hear you... Hector and I are over at this all-white-day party at Ibiza. TTYL! Love you babes."

Alisa rolled her eyes, threw her phone down on her bed and started getting ready for her night out with Sean. Deep inside, Alisa was nervous and having second thoughts, as she thought about her current relationship. But on the other hand, she wanted to go through with meeting Sean to see if they had more than just a physical attraction. To calm her nerves and kill some time, she tried to catch up on her favorite talk show "The Wendy Williams Show." She laughed and said to herself, I sure wish I were in the audience so I could be part of the "Ask Wendy" segment. After catching up on hot topics, she threw on her favorite pair of XOXO white jeans that hugged her perfectly, a tight, deep-V white-tee, and her white stiletto Nine West sandals. She headed out looking like a million bucks.

Maggiano's Little Italy was buzzing. The beautiful popular restaurant was packed, the food delicious, and they shared good conversation, laughs, and plenty of palm-sweating chemistry. The date ended well with another lingering hug, and led to an anticipated juicy passionate kiss. They were both excited and couldn't wait to see one another again.

Sean was a man not to wait to schedule another date, so he asked her on the spot to meet up at happy hour on Thursday. He said he wished he could see her again tomorrow, but his work schedule was looking crazy and he wouldn't be off until Thursday. Alisa agreed and was too thrilled that he wanted to see her again so soon.

In the meantime, Alisa and Sean communicated every day. He greeted her with good morning texts and signed off with good night notes as well. They facetimed and talked like they had been friends forever. But everything wasn't just simple peaches and cream for Alisa. It was becoming scary. She hadn't felt so connected with someone in years. One evening, she was at home after work, and just sat there on the couch, pondering over what she should do about her relationship with Derrick. She was wondering if she should tell him they should take a break. And she was trying to decide if she should tell Sean about her current situation—he didn't even know that there was a situation! Alisa had wanted to tell him that night at Maggiano's, but couldn't find the words. ...And Derrick had been more attentive and trying to spend more time with her. What to do? She was enjoying the distraction of her new sexy friend, Sean, who she was physically and intellectually attracted to. And she didn't want to hurt anyone. Not much later, Derrick came home and interrupted her internal debate by walking in with a bunch of white Calla Lilies, her favorite flowers. "Get dressed, sexy teacher," he said. "We're going out tonight. I know I've been tripping lately and I want to treat my lady to a night on the town."

But almost the whole time they were out at dinner, Alisa couldn't stop thinking about Sean. The glasses of Myx Moscato and thoughts of Sean had Alisa all turned on. ...They left the restaurant and Alisa, somewhat buzzed, instructed Derrick to feed her his dick. She was feeling really naughty and leaned over to give Derrick a treat.

Derrick was driving his red Corvette and, he sped down the highway trying to get Alisa home quick, not quite realizing how fast he was going or that a police car was posted up on the side of the road. He saw headlights appear behind them minutes later and those lights turned into bright red and blue flashing lights. Derrick and Alisa were trying to figure out where that cop car came from while they pulled over. They both franticly tried to fix themselves to look normal. The officer approached. Derrick rolled down his window.

"Do you know why I'm pulling you over?" the officer asked.

"I think it's because I might've been driving a little over the speed limit," Derrick replied. "But I honestly didn't realize how fast I was going."

The officer asked for Derrick's license and registration. Derrick leaned across Alisa to get out his registration. He then went into his wallet for his license. He started to panic when he didn't see it anywhere. He also realized his fly was still down. The officer looked concerned and asked him if he had been drinking because he thought he smelled alcohol on his breath. The officer then told Derrick to step out of the car. Alisa looked over thinking this couldn't be happening!

Derrick was scared that he could possibly go to jail because he had been drinking, driving without his license, and speeding. He got out of the car, but so did Alisa. The officer asked Derrick to walk in a straight line. While he attempted to, Alisa walked around to where they were and as she approached them, she realized that the officer looked like her new friend, Sean. The officer looked over and saw her face. He recognized that it was Alisa. It was a very awkward moment for both of them. Alisa didn't know what to say or do, praying that Sean wouldn't say anything to Derrick about her and him seeing each other. She quickly asked Sean if she could speak with him for a few minutes. They walked a few steps away from Derrick to talk.

Alisa said right away, "I am so sorry I hadn't told you I was seeing someone. I wanted to but I was waiting for the right time and I'm not sure if I even still wanted to be with him anymore. And it's not because of you, there are other issues. I really like you and want us to see where our friendship goes."

Sean replied, "I understand. We just met and to be honest with you, even if you told me you were with someone, I would've still pursued you because of our magnetic connection and you're just beautiful inside and out—look at that face and body. I tell you what, I'll let your drunk-ass friend slide this time as long as you drive home. And I hope to still be able to see you on Thursday."

Alisa was shocked and appreciative, saying thank you so much and that she owed him. Alisa told Derrick that the officer agreed to let her drive home and that Derrick was getting a get out of jail free card. Now he was confused as to what just happened, and why in the hell Alisa had gotten out of the car to talk to the officer in the first place. When she walked to the driver's side of the car she asked Derrick to move to the passenger's seat because she was going to have to drive. Derrick exited the car and yelled, "What the fuck was that about Alisa? I can speak for myself! What made you think it was cool to do that shit, huh?"

Alisa was sitting in the driver's seat and staring at him like he had lost his damn mind. She said to him, "You need to calm your drunk-ass down, Papi, because I just saved your ungrateful ass from getting a ticket and going to jail! Besame el culo!"

They went back and forth with each other, until Derrick finally came to his senses. He apologized and thanked her for thinking so fast and sweet-talking him out of going to jail. "I'm sorry my Puerto Rican princess. You had my back and I am definitely appreciative. I wish I had you with me the other two times I got pulled over and was ticketed."

Alisa laughed and replied, "You better be appreciative, big head! And you can sober up some while I drive us home, so you'll be able to show me just how grateful you are." They both laughed as she drove off. Derrick agreed to handle that.

Once home, Derrick jumped in the shower to get himself nice and fresh so he would be ready to put it down. Alisa quickly got undressed and laid there anxious, while thinking about how extremely sexy Sean looked in his uniform. Mr. Officer, that's what she decided to call him. She started to fantasize about Sean putting her on his car, turning her around with her back facing him, putting his handcuffs on her and then pressing her against the car. She thought about him lifting up her dress and ripping off her panties, gripping and pulling her hair, then kissing her neck and lightly choking her while rubbing his big long thick dick on her juicy already wet kitty. Alisa was so turned on by the fantasy she started playing with herself and rubbing on her clit.

Derrick got out of the shower, saw Alisa's activity and jumped in the bed to assist. He put his hand down on her kitty and started taking over, rubbing her clit and sliding a few fingers in. Alisa moaned and lifted herself up, started kissing him passionately, grabbed his hard, fat dick and started stroking it. Derrick laid her back down, then put his face in between her legs and kissed her lower lips, and sucked on her clit while he held her stomach down with his strong, muscular, tatted-up arms so she couldn't get away. He then got on top and slid inside of her, slow grinding in and out while Alisa moaned, "Ay papi! Papi chulo! Dame un beso."

Derrick understood some Spanish, so he followed her orders and started kissing her, putting her hands up and holding them down on the bed, while he stroked and pounded her pussy knowing that she could take it. Derrick started getting into a zone and started his own moaning, growling, biting, and saying things out loud: "Girl, your pussy feels so good. Damn, I love your tight warm pussy! Damn, Denise! This is your dick!"

Alisa stopped him in mid-stroke, and yelled out, "Ay Dios Mio! You just called me Denise, your fucking ex. Maldito Pendejo! Besame el culo idiota! Get your trifflin' ass off of me!"

Derrick tried to explain, but he knew it was a lost cause. He flat out fucked up. He just apologized and went to sleep in the extra bedroom. What a way to end the night, or more accurately, start the morning. Alisa lied down on her pillow, heated and wanting to throw all of Derrick's shit out, along with his ass. After feeling a little bad about thinking of Sean, she felt better now that Derrick revealed that he's obviously still sleeping with his ex. Now Alisa was ready to see what Officer Sean was about, and she was definitely going to kick Derrick's ass to the curb. She couldn't wait to see Mr. Officer on Thursday, and she was hoping that he'd have his handcuffs with him!

Thursday, Thursday, Thursday! The day was finally here. Alisa was so excited to see Mr. Officer. Sean called Alisa and asked her if she would feel comfortable skipping the happy hour, and instead ordering dinner and having drinks at his apartment. Alisa agreed and asked him to text his address. And after work, she made her way over to his place and called him when she was out front. He went downstairs and greeted her with a big hug and kiss. He looked and smelled so yummy, his YSL cologne tickled Alisa's senses. Damn he looks delicious, Alisa thought, as she watched his sexy body bulging through his wife beater and gym shorts. They went inside his well-decorated luxury apartment and he showed her around. Alisa was quite impressed with Sean's taste. He had contemporary black leather couches complimented by unique sculptures throughout the place. They ordered Chinese and started pouring and sipping on Roscato. They talked, laughed, and when the food arrived, they ate while playfully chatting. Having a great time, they started asking each other sexual questions. Then Alisa told him about the fantasy she had about him. Sean blushed and smiled, then said, "Fantasies are cool but reality is way better!"

He eased her to him by pulling her in by her tiny waist and started kissing her, then grabbed her hair and pulled it, asking her if she would join him in his bedroom. Once there, he got out his handcuffs, put his arms around her, turned her around and cuffed her, telling Alisa she was under arrest! Alisa screamed out "Oh, yes, Mr. Officer, I've been a naughty girl. Can you please punish me? Beat me with your big, fat long dick!" Sean kissed her from behind while he had her pressed against the wall, rubbing his hands into her panties and playing with her fat, juicy treasure box! They both moaned with excitement and pleasure while he took down her panties, bent her over, and started kissing on her soft round ass. He got on his knees and spread her massive ass cheeks and moved down to her pussy. He started to munch on her sweet treasure, like it was his last meal. He then turned her around to get better access as her fat ass blocked him from getting it the way he wanted it. He held one of her legs up placing it over his shoulder while he continued to kiss her down low. He found her clitoris and licked her pussy until Alisa's juices covered his face. She moaned loudly "Lick me faster." Sean did exactly as he was told and licked her pussy faster. Sean put two of his fingers inside her slit and licked her clit faster and faster. He felt Alisa's walls spasm around his fingers as she climaxed. He stood up, held her throat, choking her lightly, then bent her over the bed, put on a condom, and started stroking that fully juiced box! Pulling up her cuffed hands, then choking her from behind, she yelled out, "Choke me harder, Mr. Officer. Yes, I like that, harder!" He got so turned on by that he came like a volcano erupting all over her back after taking the condom off! They both lay there breathing hard and experiencing the feeling of pure ecstasy! Both saying how amazing the sex they just experienced was and wanting more of it!

"I am in sexual bliss!" Alisa said to Sean. "My fantasy was turned into an awesome reality! But can you please take these cuffs off?" They both had to laugh.

Alisa sat at home thinking of what to say to Derrick when he got back to the house. Today was the day they both agreed to sit down like two adults to discuss how to best move forward. He had been staying at his best friend Tony's house for a few days, trying to let things cool off. Alisa loved Derrick but she had fallen out of love with him. Sometimes after someone you love hurts you to your core, it's hard to forget and build back the trust. Alisa heard Derrick's car pull up to the house, she looked outside and to her surprise both her mother and his were present. Alisa was heated, not sure what to expect with the presence of both of their mothers. Derrick walked in with a teddy bear and a box of Godiva chocolates. He announced that he had some surprises for Alisa. Not amused by his gesture Alisa shot him a look of disgust. He then announced that he flew both of their mothers down for a special evening. Both moms were all smiles as they walked into the living room area where Alisa was sitting. Alisa got up and hugged both women. Derrick asked Alisa to stay standing and in a shaky voice said, "Alisa I know I haven't always made the best decisions in our relationship, but I'm ready to make things official. You have been by my side and I want you to be my wife. I think it's time we share the same last name." Both mothers gasped in excitement. Alisa's mom was in tears. There was an awkward silence as Derrick got on his knees and placed the flawless three caret pear-shaped diamond ring on Alisa's finger.

Alisa was truly speechless. The polish, symmetry, clarity and design of the ring was beautiful. She had never dreamed of ever having a ring so gorgeous. Derrick was sweating bullets from the dazed look on Alisa's face. Alisa's mom broke the silence and said "So what will it be mami?" Alisa shook her head and came right out and told everyone that their relationship wasn't working and she wanted out. She turned and apologized to her mom for what she was about to say. She said, "Derrick I wouldn't want to share a box of chocolates with you let alone your last name, no offense, Momma Joan [Derrick's mother]. You have cheated, lied, and stolen from me so many times. I'm fucking fed up. I'm keeping the ring cause I earned this. You got some nerve asking for my hand after all these years. You are one trifling asshole. Go back to your babymother."

Derrick's mother interrupted Alisa's rant and begged for Alisa's forgiveness. Derrick also chimed in and pleaded with Aliza, and he and his mother were full of tears. Alisa's mother was beyond pissed as her daughter kept her misery a secret over the years. Alisa's mom slapped Derrick in the face and said, "I think it's time for you to get your shit and get out. I believe your mother can help you pack." Momma Joan cleared her throat, and said, "My son isn't perfect but none of us are. Let these two young people figure things out." Alisa's mom looked sternly into Derrick's mother's eyes and replied, "Joan you know my princess deserves better. Think about what you went through with Derrick's father." Momma Joan ran out the room in tears. Derrick, upset with Alisa's mother, yelled, "You didn't have to go there you stupid bitch." Alisa picked up the remote control and hit him in the head with it. Her mother held her back and said to Derrick, "You are lucky I'm saved cause if I wasn't, I would beat you like you stole something." Momma Joan reentered the room after hearing the loud screams. She told her son he was too good to marry Alisa and her crazy family. She helped Derrick gather some items and they left.

Alisa's mom stayed for a week to comfort her daughter. As she headed back to New York, she demanded that Alisa never keep secrets again. Alisa did a lot of reflecting and knew she needed more time for certain wounds to heal before she could even see herself being in a steady relationship. She wanted to have her options open and date without any commitment until she felt like she was ready. She enjoyed Sean's company, and they began to become pretty close. She told him the details of what transpired with her and Derrick and was ready to get out for a night of fun. So Alisa was super excited when Sean asked her to join him for a ride along and without hesitation, she said "Ay, Papi! This will be exciting!" Sean laughed and told her, "It can be dangerous too, but I'll protect you! That's what I do!" He thought the ride along would be a perfect way to help her get her mind off things.

So they got in his squad car and headed out to the first call that came over his radio. Sean took Alisa to an apartment complex where someone had assaulted his girlfriend and the victim's 12-year-old son. Sean got out of the car and walked over to the scene in the parking lot where two other officers tried to restrain the guy. Sean jumped right in and helped get him to the ground then proceeded to get the cuffs on him. Alisa watched in amazement. She got aroused by seeing him in action with his big, strong, sexy self.

As soon as Sean got into the car Alisa told him how much he turned her on and asked him to pull over somewhere off the road and out of sight. He quickly found a spot that seemed hidden enough and put the car in park. Immediately they started kissing and removing clothes like two wild animals going at it! Alisa wanted him to take her outside and turn the flashing lights on. He did what was asked! She took down her pants, spread the top of her body onto the back end of the car, then assumed the position. Sean said to her, "Oh, you want to get cuffed, choked, and hit from the back, huh? Naughty girl."

"Yes, Mr. Officer," she replied, "in that order Papi Chulo!" Alisa reached down and unzipped Sean's pants, his massive meat sprang out as if it was impatiently waiting to be freed. He said, "Oh you want to be bad girl." He put on the cuffs, squeezed her soft breasts and caressed them, then played with her nipples until they were hard. He then pulled her up by her neck choking her slightly, kissed her and bit her bottom lip, slid his wrapped penis in her wet throbbing kitty, and beat that pussycat up! Their animal attraction and heated passion even had nearby wildlife turnin' up! Alisa said in a sexy moaning voice in her native tongue, "Mr. Officer! Ay Papi me encanta! Te sientes tan bien, el sexo es el major," while she came all over that rock hard long thick dick that was pulsating inside of her. Turned on even more by the flashing lights in the background that glowed on Alisa's beautifully positioned sexy body, Sean climaxed, grabbed her hips and held her tight while kissing and biting her neck and upper back. What a rush!

Alisa said while catching her breath, "When is the next available ride along?" They laughed and then kissed each other passionately! After that wild night, they continued to see each other and kept a great understanding in their relationship—no pressure, no commitment. Alisa made frequent distress calls to her Mr. Officer. And Sean was always there to protect and serve!

Got a Wife and a Mistress in the Basement

Sarah was one of my sweetest clients, and sometimes people truly took her sweetness for a weakness. Especially, her lowdown sneaky husband Todd. He was the worst offender of taking advantage of Sarah. From the outside they looked like the dream couple, but behind closed doors it was a nightmare...

Sarah was biracial and had pale skin, with a face full of freckles and beautiful green eyes. She was a natural redhead and always wore a smile. Sarah's mom was Caucasian; her mother's family rejected Sarah, and her younger sister, Hana. Sarah didn't have much of a family growing up. Her father passed away when she was ten, and while the DMV was home, most of her father's family lived in Atlanta. They loved Sarah and Hana but with the distance the girls didn't get a chance to really know them, especially after their father's passing.

When he was alive her dad made sure the girls knew where they came from. He would pack their mom, and his two princesses Sarah and Hana in his '82 Burgundy Honda Civic for a family road trip to Big Momma's house. Those road trips and family meals with Sarah's dirty south family stuck with her growing up as the best part of her family life. Once her dad died, finances got tight and her mom fell into a deep depression. The girls had to leave the comforts of suburban living in Clinton, Maryland, and moved to the Southview apartments in Southeast Washington, DC. Sarah's mom had to work three jobs just to keep food on the table. The girls really felt the struggle living with their mom in their one bedroom apartment. Growing up, Sarah and Hana worked hard in school and made a promise to each other to make it out the 'hood; and that's exactly what they did. Hana worked for the federal government and was a GS-14 before the age of thirty. Sarah was a dermatologist. Both sisters were college educated and fierce. Their mom was so proud of her queens, as she called them, and the girls worked together to move their mom back in the suburbs. Life was good.

Todd was also biracial but he grew up with the finer things. His mother was the first African-American nurse to work at the Washington Hospital Center, and his father was a Jewish lawyer. He grew up with nannies and trips to Paris each spring. He had an exotic look, with beautiful caramel skin, straight jet-black hair and dark brown slanted eyes. His friends used to call him chink. Growing up, Todd always felt the need to prove himself to others. His African-American peers would tease him and call him pretty boy and soft. He ended up in a lot of trouble for fighting throughout his school years because of the name-calling. His parents, frustrated with his behavior, decided to send him to military school. That was the best thing for him. Todd left a boy and came back a man.

He attended Howard University as an undergrad and stayed on the dean's list. It was during his sophomore year that Todd met his soul mate, though at first, he didn't even realize it. He had class with this beautiful, bushy-headed, red-haired girl name Sarah. Sarah was brilliant and got straight A's on all the chemistry exams. Todd struggled with chemistry and recognized he needed help. He also recognized Sarah's intelligence and asked if she could help him with an upcoming chemistry final. The two studied together for days. And not only was Sarah smart but she had a great sense of humor. She made Todd laugh and he learned like never before. The pair became the best of friends. Sarah faced many financial troubles throughout the years, but Todd, her knight in shining armor, always had her back. She thought she was going to have to quit school to work fulltime her senior year, but Todd had a powerful family with many connections and he was able to help Sarah get funding through a donor pool. He felt like he had to help his friend financially, as she had done for him regarding his studies. When things got tight for Sarah he always came to her rescue. And while she supported him, she never understood why he had supported her because she and Todd were just friends. They never even kissed. Sarah barely had money for books so her fashion and hair was just so-so. Her roommate Lisa would let her borrow some dresses during homecoming or for parties, but other than that, Sarah was just what most would call plain. She had a natural beauty but really lacked the confidence of other girls.

Todd was the lady's man on campus. The ladies of HU loved them some Todd. Sarah would just laugh at all the stories he shared with her regarding the girls he hooked up with. Some of them wanted to fight Sarah because she was the one constant in Todd's life. Girls would come and go but the two best friends were always together. The besties graduated Howard with honors and went on to medical school together. During one late-night study session during medical school, Sarah was studying alone and got an unexpected visit from Todd. He was a mess and in tears about this big-booty chick named Jessica who dumped him for an older guy. Todd bought Jessica whatever she wanted and worshiped the ground she walked on. As always, Sarah was there to comfort her friend, in that moment a light bulb went off in Todd's head. He silently thought, "Why am I out here chasing women and getting used when I have a queen by my side? What a fool I am." Todd made a promise to himself that day that he would win Sarah's heart beyond her seeing them only as friends. She would be his lady. And he would make her his wife.

Todd did exactly as he said he would. He showed Sarah a whole new world. He professed his love to her and spoiled her rotten. He updated her closet and filled it with designer everything; you name it he got it for her. He took her to his hairstylist cousin to get her hair done faithfully every two weeks. Sarah transformed from a caterpillar to a butterfly. Instead of wearing her typical boot-cut baggy jeans and sweaters, she was showing her curves in jeggings and Burberry fitted shirts. She was a bad chick. When Sarah now walked in the room people took notice. Her long flowing red hair was a head turner. After graduating medical school, the two decided to get married and opened a dermatology practice together. From the outside, Sarah looked like she had it all. But deep down inside, she still lacked the confidence and Todd, who wasn't quite so loving, used that to his advantage. Todd felt he was responsible for the change in Sarah. He had bought her everything she owned and basically paid her way through school. With Todd she instantly went from rags to riches. And he knew it.

Todd was happy to finally be in a relationship where he felt in control. He had a tight hold on Sarah, and he had begun to abuse it. When her sister Hana graduated from Morgan State, Hana wanted to take a weekend trip to Miami. When Todd heard his beloved Sarah on the phone talking to Hana about Miami he lost it. He ripped the phone out of the wall and forbade her from going. He said respectable married women don't go on trips with single women. She should only go on trips with her husband.

Sarah begged and begged for Todd to let her go. "It's my sister," she said, but he denied her request. When she mentioned that his mother went on vacations with her girlfriends, Todd turned bright red and slapped Sarah's face. She knew then and there that she was not married to the Todd she thought she married. Sarah cried and cried and never spoke of the trip or any other weekend getaway to her husband again. She told her sister she had to speak at some dermatologist convention the weekend of Hana's Miami trip and left it at that. She knew she had a comfortable life with Todd and needed to be the good wife.

Todd on the other hand took multiple trips with the fellas, going to the Super Bowl games, Vegas to the Mayweather fights, and the NBA All-Star weekends. Very rarely did he take Sarah to major events. He said he didn't think she would be interested. She was only allowed to attend if his friends took their wives. For Todd, it was OK for him to hang with his friends but for Sarah it was forbidden. She was only allowed to go to work and come back home. If Sarah took a detour to the store and didn't report it to Todd, he would beat her. One time there was a traffic jam on Route 210 and Sarah got home seven-minutes late. Todd greeted her with his timer and a belt. He beat her like a runaway slave. With Sarah being so fair skinned the bruises showed. She would make up all sorts of excuses to cover up the torment she experienced at home.

The office was the only space Sarah had control over. She ran their dermatology business like a true boss. She had grown their operations and it was the top dermatologist office in the DMV. All the local celebrities visited: Wizard ballers, Redskins, radio personalities. You name them, they were there. She put her all into their practice and felt fully in control until the day Todd hired Tasha as their nurse assistant.

Tasha and Sarah had a physical resemblance, even more than Sarah and Hana. Patients just knew that Tasha and Sarah were sisters. Tasha stood five foot seven, with killer curves. She was also very pale with freckles. She wore her hair straight with a middle part down her back, just like Sarah. Her hair was even the same shade of red. It was really strange that Todd would hire someone who looked exactly like his wife. Sarah certainly thought so.

Sarah was totally against Todd's latest hiring selection. There was something about Tasha that didn't sit right with Sarah. She actually felt like Todd was trying to have this trick take her place, and Tasha was ready for her spot. Sarah, meanwhile, knew there really wasn't anything she could do to get rid of Tasha. Sarah just kept her eyes open and tried to put on a front to find out as much information as she could about little Miss Tasha.

One May afternoon, Sarah got a text from her sister Hana stating she had something important to show her, but before she could share it Sarah had to promise not to tell Todd. Sarah promised, and a few minutes later she received a slew of text messages with photos of Tasha and Todd sitting ringside at a Floyd Mayweather fight in Las Vegas. Directly after those were photos of Tasha and Todd leaving a famous clothing boutique in Vegas named Devanna Love. Sarah could not believe her eyes and threw the phone across the room. She was devastated by what she saw. Her husband was supposed to be in Vegas with his boys, yet he was out treating Tasha to all the luxuries Sarah worked so hard to create. Sarah felt so disrespected, she wanted so badly to confront her lying husband but instead she decided to just play along as she always did, and as she promised her sister she would. Sarah had been faithful for years. She knew her husband played around. Heck, they couldn't have children because of the diseases he brought home to her. But for Sarah's own sister to bring the news to her hurt and truly embarrassed her. The fake image Sarah was putting out to the world of her perfect marriage was ruined. Hana was in Vegas with several of their childhood friends and everyone was there to witness what Todd was doing. Sarah knew she had to do something to get Tasha away from her husband.

When Todd came home from Vegas, Sarah happily greeted her husband just like a good wife should. She had on a sexy white lace bra and panty set and was adding the finishing touches to his favorite meal. She had purchased his favorite bottle of wine and set the mood. After dinner, Todd thanked Sarah for being so good to him. Sarah felt an intense heat come over her body, as she so badly wanted to blurt out, yeah, well why are you fucking our nurse and treating her like you should be treating me? Instead of playing into her impulse, she got on all fours and crawled over to her husband like an obedient puppy and unzipped his pants. She took his semi-soft penis into her mouth. She licked and sucked until it grew stiff and hard like a rock. Her tongue moved up and down his shaft. He then pushed Sarah back and said in a strong tone, "Take that shit off now!" Sarah complied with her husband's demand, and Todd went straight to her love zone, and licked her pussy juices for thirty-minutes straight, sucking and stabbing her pussy with his tongue. Sarah came about three times— her pussy pulsated as her juices flowed from having multiple organisms. Sarah's feelings of anger had disappeared as Todd entered her and took her to heaven with each stroke. Sarah was truly dick whipped. Todd was her first love. He didn't always treat her the best, but he was all she knew.

About a month went past after Sarah discovered the affair Todd was having with Tasha. Sarah just pushed it into the back of her mind. She was determined to save her marriage and just turned a blind eye, until the day Todd did the unthinkable. One day Sarah came home early and saw both Tasha's and Todd's cars in the driveway. She had a headache after realizing both of their schedules were cut early for the day. She sat in her BMW for a few minutes but knew she had to go inside. When she opened the front door, Tasha was in her kitchen cooking. Sarah walked in and said, "Hi, Tasha. Where is *my husband*?"

Tasha said "Oh, hello Sarah. He is upstairs taking a shower. He asked that I get started on dinner as he has something very important to share with you."

"Oh really," replied Sarah. "Something like what?"

Tasha smiled as she stirred the pot. "I think it may be best if Todd told you."

As if summoned, Todd appeared in the dining room wearing his towel. He walked up to Sarah and gave her a passionate kiss. He said, "Hi baby, I know you are probably wondering why Tasha is here. Well, I offered Tasha the guest room in the basement until she gets on her feet. See Tasha is having problems with her boyfriend and I thought it would be good for her to stay here. She can keep you company when I'm away."

Sarah was full of anger and disgust, and said to Todd, "Can I speak to you in the dining room, please?"

They walked into the dining room and Sarah went HAM. She yelled at Todd, "What in the fuck is wrong with you!? You have lost your damn mind! You think its OK to tell someone they can stay here without even discussing it with me first? You're being so disrespectful right now!"

Todd slapped her face before she could say another word. He then grabbed her by her arms and shook her, and slammed her into the wall. He said to her in a low, stern voice, "Don't loose *your* fucking mind. Don't I give you everything? Don't I show you love and affection? You love living this life, and being in this home, and driving these cars? Look at me: Tasha is staying here until she gets a place of her own. There's nothing else to discuss. Are we understood, Sarah, my lovely obedient wife? ..."

Sarah felt so small and enslaved at this point. She just agreed with Todd so that he wouldn't hurt her anymore. She knew now that something needed to change in her life because she couldn't continue to live like this and take the shit that Todd kept serving. He already embarrassed her by being seen out of town, sitting cozy with Tasha by Sarah's sister and some of their mutual friends. Now he had the nerve and audacity to bring that heffa into their home to sleep under her roof? And cooking in her kitchen? Oh, hell naw! Sarah had reached her limit with Todd's ass! She was going to play along with his sick and twisted plans for now, but she was thinking of her own master plan. The rest of that night was uncomfortable and quiet.

The new houseguest was making it uncomfortable for Sarah to relax in her own home. Most days, she wanted to go home after a long day at work to try to have peace of mind and unwind, but that had not been happening for the last few weeks. Then weeks turned into months. And Tasha had started to get her mail sent to their address, too.

As more time went by, Sarah actually started to become comfortable with the situation. Again, she had started letting her insecurities and her weakness for Todd take control. She knew that he and Tasha were having sex in their marital home behind her back, but she still hadn't caught them in the act. She needed a miracle. That's when Sarah's sister, Hana, came to visit unexpectedly one Saturday morning. She had been trying to reach Sarah but hadn't heard from her for weeks so she came over to make sure that her big sis was OK.

To Hana's surprise, Tasha answered the door! Hana said to her, "What are you doing here answering my sister's door, and where is my sister?" Tasha told her that she had been staying there and that Sarah was in the kitchen. Hana was disturbed by the information, and couldn't help but notice the protruding belly that Tasha was sporting. Hana was upset and wanted to blurt out some things but kept them to herself. She entered the kitchen and Sarah was shocked and embarrassed to see her. She gave her sister a hug then started tearing up in her arms. Sarah missed Hana so much and really wanted to talk to her about everything that had been going on, but Todd put fear in her heart.

Hana looked into Sarah's face and said, "Sis, come with me, get your things and let's get out of here. We need to talk, and not anywhere in or around this house. Where is Todd?"

"He's out playing basketball with his friends. I'll have to tell him I'm leaving the house so he won't be mad at me," Sarah exclaimed.

"Bump that shit," Hana answered. "Come on, we're leaving now!"

They left out and Hana drove to a coffee shop named Coffee Connection, not far from Sarah's house. They ordered and sat at a cozy little table in the corner. Hana asked, "What in the hell is going on Sarah? Why is Tasha staying in your home, and why does that bitch look pregnant?"

Sarah cried and told her everything. She told her that she thought that Tasha had picked up some weight, that's all. Hana was tired of Sarah being so naive, because she knew that she was smarter than that and not blind. Hana yelled at her sister and told her how disappointed she was in her! The patrons in the coffee shop all stopped and tuned into the sisterly conversation. Hana lowered her voice and told Sarah that a friend of hers is a private detective and she would get him to put cameras throughout the house and audio recorders as well, so that Sarah could get the evidence she needed to take Todd to court for a divorce and half of everything she's entitled to.

"It's time for you to get rid of his lying, cheating, possessive, abusive ass for good!" Hana said. Sarah agreed to let Hana's friend come to the house with her to set things up.

A few days later, Todd, Sarah, and Tasha were all at work, when Sarah said she wasn't feeling well. Todd told her to go home and take something and lay back. Of course, he didn't mind her doing that for more than one reason. He knew that she was obedient and didn't think that she'd lie to him to sneak around, and he'd have the chance to play a little with his mistress in his office after hours.

Sarah was nervous and feeling subconscious, but left and headed home. She called Hana and told her to meet her at the house and not to waste any time. Hana arrived with her friend, Russ, she introduced him, they greeted each other and they were ready to get to work. Russ asked Sarah what room should he start in? Sarah said without him even finishing the question, "the basement!" Russ and the sisters went through the house making sure everything was being placed and hidden properly. Sarah was feeling nervous and she was ready for them to leave before Todd and Tasha popped up to the house and saw them there, especially when she should be sick in bed. They finished the last room and Hana gave Sarah a hug and kiss on her cheek and told her, "Everything is going to work out for you big sis, don't worry. You'll get the evidence that you need. I hope you can handle what you'll see and hear. You deserve better." Hana then added a bit more, realizing that Sarah's life was about to change in a big way. "Material things aren't everything. He stopped respecting you a long time ago, and treats you like his pet. You won't be losing anything; you'll definitely be gaining. Love yourself, sis, and know I love you, too. Pray and stay strong."

Sarah was like a kid waiting for the new Jordan's to be released. She couldn't wait to see how the equipment was going to work out. She had a hunch her trifling husband was disrespecting their home with that slut, but to see it on camera and take it to court would give her the extra boost she needed to finally let him go. Sarah replayed her sister's pep talk in her head and made a promise to herself to pay attention to detail, to love herself and to no longer be blinded by fear. Sarah always had a deep fear of being alone and stuck with bills, struggling like her mom did once her dad passed. Sarah said a prayer, held on tightly to the dainty gold cross that adorned her neck, and repeated her promise to herself again as reassurance. Just as she finished her promise, Todd and Tasha came home together like a loving couple. Sarah was so empowered she didn't even let their closeness get to her as usual. She had a plan in place and was determined to follow through on her promise.

A few days went by and Sarah was anticipating what would be revealed. She started paying more attention and saw that Tasha's stomach was becoming noticeably larger and decided to ask her what was up with it. Sarah asked, "What's going on with your stomach girl? You've always kept yourself in great shape. Looks like somebody's slippin' a bit."

Tasha let out a laugh and replied, "Sarah, thanks for your concern, but me and my belly are just fine. I will handle mine, and you handle yours. I'm going to go down to my room and chill. Is there anything else you want to say to me, or are you done?"

Sarah's face was frowned all the way up, she didn't want to argue with her and bring Todd into it, so she just walked away shaking her head without saying another word.

That night, Todd had been impatiently waiting to creep down to their basement for one of him and Tasha's regular routine sex sessions. After Sarah finally fell asleep, Todd tiptoed down the stairs and tapped on the door to Tasha's room. She let him in and he immediately kissed her passionately and started taking off her sheer nighty, and seeing that she was not wearing any panties. He got excited and laid her on the bed then went head first into her plump juicy lower lips, kissing, licking, sucking, and savoring all of her natural juices until she came. Tasha moaned with pleasure and told Todd that she loved how he kissed her and always made sure she came first. Then Todd played with her clit some more while he sucked on her full, round breasts. She grabbed him and kissed him deeply, sucking on his tongue and grabbing his large thick juicy pole, stroking up and down on it. She spit on it and continued to stroke it, running her hands up and down the length, admiring the size. She slowly licked every inch of his dick. Then she sucked on his head for a moment, massaging his meat with her mouth. Tasha gazed into Todd's eyes and said, "don't worry baby I swallow unlike your bitch of a wife." Todd loved when Tasha made comparisons to what Sarah wouldn't or couldn't do. He chuckled and grabbed her head putting his erect penis deep in her mouth. Tasha deep throated his dick as he pushed her head down further and further. Tasha gagged on it and Todd's lap soon was soaked from the fluids running from her mouth. Todd grabbed her up by her throat and choked her then pulled her in kissing her as he gripped her neck. He entered her and they fed off of each other's chemistry, kissing and grinding, massaging and caressing, until Todd climaxed. They lay there on the bed together trying desperately to catch their breath.

As Todd held on to Tasha from behind, and while softly rubbing on her stomach, he said with emotion, "I am so in love with you. Our sex is the best I've ever had. Maybe it's gotten better because you're pregnant with my baby. You're giving me something I always wanted and never had. You and our unborn child mean everything to me. I'll make sure you're always taken care of no matter what! I love you!"

"I love you too! I'm glad to be having your baby," Tasha replied as she teared up. "I only want for us to be a real family. Sarah needs to go. You have to get rid of her, Todd. Get a divorce because I can't continue to live like this and I'm not raising our child in this home with that bitch still in it! You need to make a decision, us or her."

Todd promised he would, but when the time was right. At that point, he said he would let Sarah know that he wasn't happy with her anymore and would file for a divorce. But he told Tasha that they had to be careful, that Sarah couldn't find out about them or the baby on the way, until they were separated. Tasha let him know that this was his only chance because she'd have no choice but to leave.

He left Tasha and tiptoed back up the stairs, washed off in the bathroom then climbed back into bed with Sarah, as if he had just simply went to use the bathroom in the middle of the night. Unknown to Todd, the sounds of his basement lovemaking session with his mistress woke his wife. Sarah was in their marital bed thinking how she couldn't wait to review the tape.

The next morning Sarah made up a lie and told Todd and Tasha she was going to stay behind, as she still was feeling ill. Actually she really was feeling a little ill as her stomach was in knots in anticipation of what she was about to view. Shortly after they pulled off she sat in her office with the door locked and pulled up some of the video. Her palms were sweating as she hit play. She started with the footage from Tasha's room and hit the jackpot on the first try. She saw the beginning of Todd and Tasha's lovemaking and couldn't stand to look any further. She was crushed and filled with anger. She knew that she still needed to listen to the audio, and she thought that she could stand that more than watching them in action. She played the audio and cried the whole time she listened, hearing everything that was said. Sarah was in a state of shock and disgust! She felt like she was stabbed in the gut, especially since Tasha was giving him what she so desperately wanted to give him but couldn't because of the internal damage that Todd's filthy cheatin' ass had caused.

She called her sister Hana and told her about everything! Hana hurried over to pick up a copy of the video for safekeeping. She also told her sister she was going to make an extra copy so there would be no flat tires in their plan to take Todd down.

Sarah told her that she didn't know if she would be able to keep her composure when he came home.

But Hana replied, "Sis, you gotta do what you gotta do. Keep it under control. The evidence is concrete, so handle your business. Once you show this video in divorce court you can take his ass to the cleaners. In fact, you might want to call Judge Mablean out of retirement for this girl. He better be ready to give you half. Truth be told, you deserve more than half. You got his ass through college and medical school. If it weren't for you, he wouldn't be shit. I support you and I will always have your back." She hugged her sister tightly and said, "I Love you."

Sarah cried and told Hana she loved her too, and thanked her for building her back together. Sarah took a hot bath, watched some soaps and sipped several glasses of wine, patiently waiting for the two lovebirds to return from work. The wine had her feeling nice and she drifted into a deep sleep.

Sarah awoke from the much-needed afternoon nap and walked downstairs to see Tasha sitting in her favorite spot on the couch, wearing a low-cut nightgown. Tasha was leaning over Todd, exposing her full breast and whispering something in his ear. Todd was all smiles. Sarah became filled with rage and flipped out! Sarah ran over to them and punched Todd in the face, then picked up a lamp from the end table and cracked him over the head. The blow knocked him out and left him lying on the floor. She kicked him violently as Tasha tried to pull her off of him, then Sarah punched her in the face and pulled her by her hair. She threw more punches, and then they both fell to the floor and went at each other like animals! Outside, one of the neighbors walking their dog heard the shouting and screaming, and called the police. Tasha broke loose and ran out the front door as Sarah chased her and swung on her some more!

The police arrived in no time to find Tasha fighting to get away from Sarah's clutch! A few officers struggled to pull them apart and put them both in cuffs as they tried to figure out what was going on. They entered the home to find Todd lying in the middle of the floor. As he came to he started asking what was going on and heard Sarah in the background yelling, "Cheater! Lying trifling' asshole! Sleepin' with that bitch that's trying to be me and take over my life!" Todd told the officers that Sarah was insecure and crazy. He said she suspected that he cheated with his assistant Tasha, but that she was just delusional. She had never seen them together. To his surprise, Sarah invited the officers to view the proof of her little secret. She took them into her home-office and showed them and let them hear the video evidence.

Todd realized now that he was ruined. And in that moment, it was the first time that he felt weak and that Sarah was in fact strong and in control.

Sarah laughed, saying, "I'll see you and your family in court bitch! Oh, and don't worry, I will be filing for a divorce and taking everything I can from you, you fucking monster! You've taken from me for so many years, now it's my turn! Let's see how that works out for you. And put some ice on that bump, it looks like it needs some medical attention."

Needless to say, Sarah went out with a bang. The moral of the story—don't loose your life trying to live someone else's. It's better to have your own things, than to take what's borrowed from others.

Meet the Authors

 Jade Badd and Renee Love are cousins on a mission to jointly bring exciting, seductive stories to readers. Supporting one another with each endeavor they have initiated, they decided to work together and turn their passion as storytellers into a business. They are overjoyed in having launched their publishing company Gurl Talk Publications, and look forward to sharing enticing stories with book lovers around the world. Learn more about this dynamic duo. …

Jade Badd

Jade is a mother, wife, author, and stylist. She is a licensed cosmetologist, and also considered a part-time "therapist"—many of her clients call her that as they confide in Jade while seeking her advice, which she eagerly provides. Not because she has to, but because of her desire to serve others. Clients say they know they can speak freely without being judged.

Although doing hair pays the bills, she's involved with a range of business interests. In early 2014, Jade used her creativity and giving nature to launch the Naughty or Nice t-shirt line—shirts are designed with positive and empowering messages. Her passion, however, is in being an author (she loves writing short stories) and songwriter. Jade has published many songs, and with this book she is pleased to share her spirit with an even broader audience.

A native of Prince Georges County, Maryland, Jade resides in the DMV area, with her husband and two daughters.

Renee Love

Renee is an author, mother, wife, fashionista, entrepreneur, and philanthropist. She's the owner of VIP Divas, an online clothing boutique, but still takes time to give back to her community. Renee has always had the unique ability to connect with people, and doing charitable work has always been a huge part of her life. From the time she was a teenager, her friends and family have come to her for advice. Polished for Prom, Dream Girls Mentoring Program, Prince Georges County Public Schools and The Red Cross are just a few of the organizations that she has served. In 2014, she even broadened her influence to launch networking events for women in business.

Renee holds a Bachelor's of Arts degree in Business Administration from Morgan State University and a Masters in Human Resources from Bowie State University. A native of Prince George's County, Maryland, Renee resides in Southern Maryland, with her husband and two children.

www.ingramcontent.com/pod-product-compliance
Lightning Source LLC
Chambersburg PA
CBHW060821250626
47162CB00005B/1884